HOW TO
FALL IN
LOVE WITH
A MAN
WHO LIVES
IN A BUSH

HOW TO FALL IN LOVE WITH A MAN WHO LIVES IN A BUSH

A Novel

emmy abrahamson

HARPER

NEW YORK • LONDON • TORONTO • SYDNEY

HARPER

FIRST EDITION

Designed by Leydiana Rodriguez

© Emmy Abrahamson, 2016
First published by Albert Bonniers Förlag, Stockholm, Sweden.

Published in the English language by arrangement with Bonnier Rights, Stockholm, Sweden.

Library of Congress Cataloging-in-Publication Data has been applied for.

ISBN 978-0-06-267803-4 (pbk.)

18 19 20 21 22 LSC 10 9 8 7 6 5 4 3 2 1

HOW TO
FALL IN
LOVE WITH
A MAN
WHO LIVES
IN A BUSH

1

I love cock!" the woman says cheerfully.

I look down at my notes, scribble something illegible, place the ballpoint on the table, and clear my throat.

"What you're trying to say . . . I think . . . or I hope . . . although I'm happy for you if you really feel that way . . . is perhaps that you love to cook. *To cook*. Not . . . *cock*."

It's the eleventh lesson of the day, and I'm so tired I've started rambling. What's more, I've spent the whole time looking down at my mint-green information card to remind myself what the student's name is. *Petra, Petra, Petra*. Worryingly, I also notice that I've taught this student at least three times before. And yet I have no memory of her. It's as though all my students have turned into a single, faceless blob that's unable to distinguish between Tuesday and Thursday and stubbornly refuses to use the perfect tense. A blob that continues to say "Please" in reply to a thank you, despite my hundreds of reminders about saying "You're welcome." A blob that believes language learning is a process that occurs automatically as long as you're in the same room as a teacher.

With a quick glance at the clock, I realize there are still another twenty minutes till the lesson is over. Twenty minutes of eternity.

"And, er . . . Petra, what kind of food do you like to cook?" I ask.

It was never my dream, or plan, to become an English teacher. But after four months' unemployment, the ad saying that Berlitz was looking for teachers was almost too good to be true. The training course was only two weeks long, and as soon as we were finished we could start teaching. Even so, I spent the first few weeks glancing at the door and expecting the ponytailed guy who'd run the course to come rushing in and breathlessly exclaim, "It was only a joke. Of course you're not allowed to teach. We were just kidding!" before throwing me out onto the street and escorting the student to safety. That was when I was still sitting up late every evening preparing the next day's lessons. I carefully drew up lesson plans, making sure each class was varied and entertaining. I made copies of interesting articles, wrote down questions, drafted inoffensive role-plays, and laminated photos that would lead into relevant themes for discussion. All to get my students speaking as much English as possible.

Now they're lucky if I even glance at their information cards before entering the room. This minor rebellion on my part started the day I realized I'd been teaching for significantly longer than the six months I'd planned and—even worse—that I was good at it. I was both patient (who'd have thought that would be the main ingredient for a good language teacher?) and had a knack for getting my students to speak English. Now that I've stopped planning my lessons and they've become a mystery to both me and my students, life has become a bit more exciting.

"Oh, everything. Schnitzel, sausages . . ." says Petra.

"Complete sentences," I say, encouragingly.

"I like to cook schnitzel and sausages," Petra says obediently.

Because the basic rule of the Berlitz method is that you can learn a language through everyday conversation, I can keep a lesson going for as long as I can come up with things to talk about. My three years as an English teacher have turned me into an expert in small talk. Once I got a student to talk for a quarter of an hour about the lock he'd changed on his garage door, just to see if I could.

"And what's your favorite drink?" I ask.

Petra considers. "Tap water."

"Complete sentences," I repeat with a strained smile.

"My favorite drink is tap water," Petra says.

I continue to smile at her, because I genuinely have no idea what to say to someone whose favorite drink is tap water.

For the final fifteen minutes, we do a cooking-themed crossword. When the bell rings I let out a little pretend sigh and turn down the corners of my mouth to show how sad I am that we have to finish. We shake hands, of course, and Petra disappears off home, probably to a dinner consisting of schnitzel and sausages washed down with a glass of tap water.

Everyone crams into the tiny staffroom so as to avoid any contact with the students during the five-minute break. On the walls there are Berlitz posters with multicultural faces and sentences followed by exclamation marks. The three bookshelves are full of Berlitz's in-house magazine, *Passport*, and some Spanish, French, and Russian textbooks that appear to be completely untouched. The English books, on the other hand, are so battered that most of them are missing their spines or are held together with tape.

None of the Berlitz staff are real teachers. Mike's an out-of-work actor, Jason's finishing his PhD on Schönberg, Claire used to work in marketing, Randall's a graphic designer, Sarah's a civil engineer, Rebecca's a violin maker, Karen has a degree in media and communication, and I still dream of one day becoming an author. The only one who's a trained teacher is Ken, so he's hated almost as much as Dagmar, the administrator at our Berlitz branch on Mariahilferstrasse.

Ken stalks into the staffroom. "Ooh, busy, busy," he says cheerfully, trying to squeeze his way through to the photocopier while holding open a grammar book. Everyone ignores him. At the window, Mike and Claire huddle together, trying to smoke through a gap of about a centimeter.

"Now I have four classes in a row with the same group." Claire sighs, stuffing her lighter back into her cigarette pack. "I won't be done until eight."

"Just a little longer and you'll never have to do this again," Randall says. Claire will be going back to London soon to do a master's.

"I'm about to have my twelfth class," I say, and an impressed murmur goes round the room. There are only three topics of conversation in the staffroom: how many classes we have to teach that day, how annoying our students are, and how much we hate Dagmar.

"I just had an AMS group," counters Mike.

Everyone sighs in sympathy. AMS is the Austrian employment office. A few years ago, Berlitz won a state contract to provide English lessons to every unemployed person who applied for them. There are few things more depressing than teaching an AMS group.

The last student of the day is new. She's already in the room when I come in, standing looking out of the dirty window. To my relief I see that her English has been classified as Level Five—that is, "A high level of competence." The higher the student's level, the less effort I have to make.

"Hi, my name is Julia," I say, offering my hand.

The thin woman puts out her hand, which is surprisingly warm. Within a quarter of an hour, I've learned that her name's Vera, she's originally from Graz, that she works as a PR consultant for the Austrian People's Party, and she is a single mother with an eight-year-old daughter. Unfortunately, she then starts asking *me* questions.

"Where are you from?"

"Sweden," I answer without thinking.

A crease immediately appears between Vera's eyebrows and I realize my mistake. Even though my English is both accent and error free, no one wants to hear that I'm not from an English-speaking country. Even Dagmar discreetly asked me not to mention it to the students. Rebecca once told me about the time she was moonlighting as a waitress at a barbecue restaurant in Cairns. Even though she always remembered everyone's orders, she had to pretend to write them down in her notepad because she noticed that the customers got nervous if she didn't. That's kind of how I feel every time I have to lie about where I come from.

"Swindon," I correct myself. "In England. Northern England."

Vera is still looking at me. "Isn't Swindon in the south of England? Near Bristol? I took a course there once."

I feel my cheeks and neck grow hot.

"This is another Swindon," I add quickly. "A smaller Swindon. We call it . . . mini-Swindon. So, Vera, tell me what you like to do on the weekend. What are your favorite pastimes?"

Vera continues to observe me with slight suspicion, and I think that I really ought to follow Rebecca's advice and stop having so many classes a day.

Unfortunately, Vera's English is almost perfect. But toward the end of the lesson, she says "in the end of the month" rather than "at the end of the month." I finally have an opportunity to correct her and stop feeling like a useless stage prop.

On the way home I suddenly have an idea for a book. It's so highly charged and creepy that I stop in my tracks and the hair on my arms stand on end. The story will be about an unsuccessful author who gets a job as a caretaker at an isolated hotel resort. He has to spend the whole winter there with his wife and young child. The child will be a boy. Or a girl. No, a boy. During the winter, the author begins to lose his mind due to the isolation and the evil spirits haunting the hotel. It all ends in a chaotic bloodbath. I can see it all laid out before me so clearly that it's almost frightening. The blizzard whining round the building, the deserted corridors, the hotel rooms where nothing moves, and the author sitting at his typewriter. What a gripping, spooky book it's going to be! I almost run home so I can start writing, and I'm astounded that no one's thought of this story before.

2

In the evening I meet Leonore at a cocktail bar in the sixth district.

I hate Leonore. In my defense, Leonore can barely stand the sight of me either, but we've both realized the symbiotic advantages our friendship offers us. Because all my other friends are in relationships and therefore turn into pumpkins at the stroke of midnight, she's the only one I can go out with, and with me, Leonore can pretend to be young and single again, instead of old and married to Gerhard, or the Beige Man as I like to call him (not in front of her).

Leonore is from England and has a son of preschool age who always wears an eyepatch for some reason. The Beige Man is the manager of Red Bull's finance department which means that Leonore never has to work again and instead she's able to devote all her time to producing, directing, and marketing plays in which she takes the lead role. Last February she played Malcolm X as part of Black History Month, sponsored by the American Embassy. Leonore's not black.

"Does Mike still work at Berlitz?" asks Leonore.

I nod and take a sip of my vodka tonic. *Fuck you, Stephen King.*

"I don't know if I should give him a part in my next play or not," says Leonore. "I'm planning on staging *Closer* by Patrick Marber. He could play Clive Owen's role."

I circle the see-through plastic stirrer between the ice cubes. I'm still bitter about Stephen King having written *The Shining* almost forty years ago, a small detail I only remembered as I put my hands to the keyboard to start typing.

"I saw Mike today, and I'm pretty sure he's sick of being an English teacher," I say. "He'd probably be really glad to get a part in *Closer*. There's a limit to how many times you can have the same lesson on the difference between the present tense and the present progressive, believe me. If I have to explain one more time why the McDonald's slogan 'I'm lovin' it' is totally unacceptable, I'm going to bang my head against a wall. God, I get so angry with McDonald's every time I think of it. So yes, you should probably give Mike a part."

If her forehead wasn't full of Botox (there are eleven years between us, after all), Leonore would have creased it now to show how much I was boring her.

"I don't know if we have the right chemistry," Leonore says.

I'm not sure whether we're still talking about Mike.

"Yeah, you probably don't have the right chemistry," I mutter, and take another gulp of my drink.

After the cocktail bar we go to Passage. The nightclub is already full of people and we have to wait behind three dark-haired girls in tiny skirts and white high heels before we can hang our coats in the cloakroom.

"Don't you think all the girls here look like high-class prostitutes from the Balkans?" I shout at Leonore over the music.

"I hope you mean us too," Leonore shouts back.

Before I can reply she pulls me to the bar. We order our drinks and pretend to talk to each other while we look at the guys. I actually have no idea why we always end up at Passage. The DJ plays unbearable music, the drinks are watered down, the bathrooms are filthy, there's nowhere to sit, and the guys are all from Germany and have girlfriends.

Within half an hour we're each standing talking to a guy. Mine has grinning sweat patches under his arms and eyebrows that meet in the middle, but he's not wholly unattractive.

"Where are you from?" he asks in German.

"Sweden," I say in English. To be honest, I can speak German, albeit with my own interpretation of the grammar, but I decide to speak English to give me the advantage.

His eyes widen and he smiles at me.

"Have you been to Sweden?" I ask.

"Nah," he says, shaking his head. "But after reading so many Swedish crime novels it almost feels like it. Sweden is Wallanderland."

"Wallanderland sounds like a theme park," I say. "One where everyone dies."

I see Leonore trying to make eye contact with me. Probably because the guy she's talking to is a head shorter than her and is wearing a necklace with a Mercedes symbol on it. Going to a nightclub in Austria often feels like being thrown back to a time when eighties jewelry wasn't worn ironically and Ace of Base still ruled. I ignore Leonore and turn back to my guy.

"A Swedish told me there's not actually any crime in Ystad," he says.

"That's because Kurt Wallander's solved all the crimes," I reply.

The guy laughs and suddenly I hope something will happen between us.

"Where are you from?" I ask.

"Munich," he replies. I tick box one.

"Do you have a girlfriend?" I ask.

The guy looks surprised at first, then smiles boyishly.

"Yeah," he says. After a few seconds, he adds: "Sorry."

I tick box two. In spite of this, I give him my phone number when he asks for it.

When I get home I watch eighties porn on RedTube and give myself an orgasm to help me sleep. But it doesn't work. I lie on my side and stare at the dark wall. I decide that next weekend I will arrange my books in color order.

3

My first group the next day is an AMS group. When I come into the room they're already sitting there like three wax dolls. There's a woman with a double chin and gold rings that cut into her fingers. A young girl with white-blonde hair and dark roots is sitting, tearing her cuticles with her teeth. The guy with a mustache and a checked shirt has a spookily absent gaze, but at least he's ready, pen in hand.

"Hi!" I say. "My name is Julia and I will be teaching you today."

None of them responds.

Once I actually had a job I loved. Just after Matthias and I moved to Vienna I got a position as a journalist. The paper was called *VIenna frOnT*—the capitals were meant to show the paper's disregard for norms and traditions. We had a tiny office in the fifteenth district and we were fueled by Almdudler soda, *Leberkäse* sandwiches, and irony. Aside from covering the domestic news, I also got to write columns about right-wing politicians' fondness for tying sweaters around their shoulders and analyses of the German-speaking world's relationship to yogurt drinks. *VIenna frOnT* was supposed to hold a mirror to the world and make it draw breath. We lasted five months before the paper went bust.

"Hello, what is your name?" I say to the woman with the sausage fingers.

"Bettina," she replies.

"My name is . . ." I correct her gently.

"My name is Bettina," she says.

Bettina's cheap, pink, butterfly-print viscose top strains over the bulges of her belly and her eyes have that desperate look that says "don't hate me." Because this group is Level Two, getting any information out of them is painfully slow. Once, an AMS student started crying when I said, "What was your last job?" Since then I've stopped asking what AMS students used to do for work, which has unfortunately halved the number of subjects we can talk about. But after three long classes, I know that Bettina gets out of bed at 4 a.m. so she can have some time to herself before her kids wake up, Steffi has a bichon frise called Toto (after the band, not *The Wizard of Oz*), and Hans likes gardening. We've also practiced common questions and greetings. All the way through I've tried to smile and be enthusiastic ("Learning a new language = NEW OPPORTUNITIES!") to avoid dashing any hope that these lessons will actually have an impact on their job hunt.

During the break, I light up when I see Rebecca in the staffroom. She walks up to me with wide eyes.

"I think one of my AMS students is drunk," she whispers and takes my arm.

"I have an AMS student who gets up at *four* every morning just to get some peace," I whisper back. "Why not just stay asleep and be undisturbed that way?"

"Four?!" mouths Rebecca.

I nod.

"But what can you even *do* at four in the morning?" Rebecca says at normal volume.

"Says she reads magazines and does sudoku," I reply, also at normal volume. Being with Rebecca always makes me happy. She's my Good Witch of the North—in contrast to Leonore who would have gotten the part of the Wicked Witch of the West if I'd been Dorothy. Rebecca and I met during the Berlitz training course and I decided she was going to be my friend as soon as I heard she was a violin maker. Someone who makes violins can only be a good, sensible person, like people who help lepers. Sadly, building violins hardly pays at all, which is why Rebecca also became an English teacher. But just think—I know someone who's a violin maker! One day I also hope to have the following friends: a lesbian, a computer geek, and someone from Brooklyn. And Elfriede, of course.

"How many lessons do you have today?" I ask.

"Just three," she replies. "With the same group. And you?"

"Ten."

Rebecca's eyes immediately narrow.

"Stop taking on so many lessons!" she says. "You should be spending your time writing books or freelance articles and interviewing people and going undercover and so on."

"But I'm undercover here," I say defensively. "I'm pretending to be an English teacher."

And with that the bell rings and I have to return for another lesson with Bettina, Steffi, and Hans.

~

With two bags of groceries in my hands I walk slowly up the stairs of the art nouveau-style building in the seventh district where I live. On the second floor, I stop and look, as I always do, at the door that leads to the flat on the left. The one that faces onto the street rather than the backyard like my fourth-floor flat. It normally smells faintly of smoke and coffee outside the door, and a few times I've glimpsed a shadow moving behind the frosted-glass windows. By the doorbell there's a little plaque that says "E. Jelinek" in ornate lettering. It took a couple of months before I realized who it could be. Then I asked the Serbian caretaker if it belonged to the celebrated novelist Elfriede Jelinek.

"Yes, yes," he nodded eagerly. "A great lady. But very shy. Doesn't go out much. Very particular."

Ever since, I've been desperately trying to bump into my famous neighbor, without success. From the street I can see that her windows are dirty even though there are some gaudy plants there. For some reason I just can't picture Elfriede Jelinek carefully tending her azaleas, however much I try. It's like my subconscious only wants to see her over-watering cactuses and feeding flies to carnivorous plants.

Sometimes I blame my neighbor for the fact that I haven't yet become an author. It's Elfriede's fault (in my rage I always address her by her first name). The building's literature quota has been used up by her, leaving nothing for me, and if Elfriede didn't live here then I'd have written at least three novels by now.

In happier times I dream of how we'll become friends. She'll come to my door to borrow a cup of vinegar.

"I'm a writer too!" I'll exclaim and Elfriede will raise her eyebrows in surprise that a colleague—and possible future soulmate—is living in the house. Then her face will become serious again.

"To observe is a male privilege," she'll say.

"Hmm," I'll agree, nodding slowly.

"My writing is a polemic against the tyranny of reality."

"But have you been to Prater? Sometimes it's pretty good fun there, Elfie," I'll say, getting a nickname in as quick as possible.

"Follow my tears and the sea will soon take you in," Elfriede will say.

"Now you've lost me, but do come in, Fifi," I'll reply—an alternative nickname, in case she didn't like the first one.

Then, over many cups of tea, or maybe whiskey, we'll sit at my place and talk about how tough it is being an author.

With a little sigh I shift my grip on the bags and carry on up the stairs. They smell of cleaning fluid and cold stone.

4

For the rest of the week I hope the German guy from Passage will call. But of course he doesn't. I pretend it doesn't matter and fill my time with teaching, going to the gym, eating uninspired meals, and watching *The Simpsons* and *Grey's Anatomy* dubbed into German. *Verdammt noch mal, Meredith, hör auf mich!* I take the train to a suburb and adopt a castrated stray cat called Optimus. With Optimus by my side I continue to eat uninspired dinners and watch attractive young doctors in Seattle fighting to save lives while learning all of life's great lessons.

Sometimes I worry that the TV series I watch are more real to me than my own life. That the love life, family, and work problems of Meredith from *Grey's Anatomy* are more tangible than my own. Sometimes I even start thinking I *am* Meredith Grey and wonder why I'm sitting explaining the difference between "some" and "any" rather than standing in an operating theater, repairing a ruptured mitral valve. Once I looked at Rebecca and got confused for a few seconds over why she wasn't Cristina Yang. And I still catch myself feeling totally crushed over the deaths of George O'Malley, Lexie Grey, and Derek Shepherd. There's not an earthquake in Turkey or a collapsed factory in Bangladesh that can bring me to tears like the fact that Denny Duquette died without Izzie at his side. He died without Izzie. Died. Without. Izzie.

One evening I was sitting at my computer about to order a set of *Grey's Anatomy* scrubs. But then I realized what kind of person I was turning into. I slammed the laptop shut and quickly rang Leonore to see if she wanted to go out. Sometimes I still dream of ordering them. Especially the short-sleeved, light-blue tunic with two front pockets and a secret pen compartment.

This evening, Rebecca is celebrating her birthday at O'Malley's at Schottentor. When I get there the pub's already full. The walls are dark green and covered with Guinness posters. I find Rebecca in the claustrophobic cellar and sit down beside her husband Jakob. Jakob is also a violin maker, and looks like Jesus. Even Jakob's brother is a violin maker, and he too looks like he's stepped out of the Bible.

"I have to tell you something," Rebecca says, leaning across Jakob. "I saw Matthias on Kaiserstrasse."

At first I say nothing. Jesus-Jakob continues to stare straight ahead.

"What was he doing?" I say finally.

"He was walking along the street," Rebecca says.

"What?" I say, my voice weak. "Just like that?"

"I know," Rebecca says, "How dare he?!"

We're interrupted by one of Rebecca's friends. I stay there beside Jesus-Jakob, thinking about Matthias.

Matthias and I were together for four years. To begin with

everything was great between us, then it was bad. We argued about him smoking too much weed and never helping with the housework. After every fight Matthias would buy me a bag of licorice as a peace offering because he knew how much I liked it. Like I was six years old.

In a last-ditch attempt to save our relationship, we decided to move to his hometown, Vienna. Everything was great between us again. I learned to say *Grüss Gott*, rediscovered Sundays, and practiced not getting run over all the time by the trams. Matthias was accepted into a photography program and because the college wanted to foster its students' understanding and respect for the fundamental creativity of photography, our new bathroom was transformed into a darkroom. The window was covered over with black trash liners and gaffer tape and my makeup jostled for space with bottles of chemicals. I bashed my head countless times on the enormous enlarger that stood between the shower and the toilet. But it didn't matter. Matthias had finally found an aim in life. He spent our paltry monthly budget on books about Mapplethorpe, LaChapelle, and Corbijn, and during the whole of his first year I was a willing model as he experimented with contrast and composition. He stopped smoking weed every day and his eyes grew clear again. Everything was okay, even when *VIenna frOnT* went bust, because Matthias's happiness came before everything else. That was back when I still believed that true love meant completely forgetting myself and only letting my moon orbit his planet. That was when I still believed I'd be the one who would save Matthias, get him to reach his full potential, and become the well-rounded being none of my friends seemed to be able to see.

The first time I realized something was wrong was during his second year in the photography program. I saw that one of Matthias's records had been left out, though it hadn't been there when we left the flat together that morning. Without giving it any more thought, I blew off the flakes of tobacco from the sleeve and put it back among the other records. Then I started noticing that the lock had only been turned once, rather than being double-locked like I always left it. And suddenly we were back to arguing almost every day and the kitchen shelf was overflowing with packages of licorice.

Then came the call. I was in bed with tonsillitis and had just been contemplating taking a nap. The telephone rang and a woman with a soft voice said they'd found one of Matthias's portfolios and wondered whether he'd like to come in and pick it up, given that he was no longer a student there.

She told me that Matthias had stopped attending classes back in October, but that it wasn't until a month ago that they'd officially taken him off their student list. It was March now. For over six months he'd been pretending to go to there every day. For over six months he'd been telling me little stories and anecdotes about things that had happened at school that day. For over six months he'd been telling me how much he was enjoying his classes and that he was looking forward to becoming a professional photographer. I almost threw up with the telephone receiver in my hand.

I immediately started searching the flat for clues. Hidden in a bag behind the panel that was loosely attached to Matthias's desktop computer I found hundreds of joint roaches. The plastic bag was carefully fastened with several elastic bands. Why he hadn't simply thrown out the roaches was a mystery. And it struck me that his textbooks were still in exactly the same order they'd been in at the start of the academic year, and that the developing trays in the bathroom had acquired a thick layer of dust.

When Matthias came home at quarter past six—after "a whole day at school!"—I confronted him. He didn't deny a thing.

"But *why*?" I asked.

"I knew how angry you'd be," he said, and in a single stroke he made it my fault.

For the last six months he'd been going to a café in the sixteenth district where the owner let customers smoke weed all day as long as they bought something to drink. If the café was closed, he'd come back to the flat as soon as I'd gone to work and then leave before I came home. It turned out Matthias was a cleaning whiz after all. At least when it came to removing all traces of what he'd been doing in the flat this whole time.

At first, every time I told someone how things ended between Matthias and me, and about his double life, I'd try and turn it into a funny anecdote. But I stopped because no one ever laughed. There's nothing funny about the story of me and Matthias.

~

After two hours at O'Malley's I make my excuses.

"It's not because I told you about Matthias?" Rebecca asks nervously.

"No, God no," I say.

When I get home I cry into Optimus's fur until he runs and hides behind the sofa.

5

I shower in the kitchen. Not because I want to shower in the kitchen, but for the simple reason that the shower is behind a little wall in the kitchen. That's how it is in most of the *Altbau* flats in Vienna. You always find the kitchen, bathroom, and toilet in the most unexpected places. In the building where Claire from Berlitz lives, in the sixteenth district, the unheated toilet is in the corridor and she has to share it with her neighbors.

When I'm showered and dressed I go to work, even though it's the weekend. I'm one of the few teachers who always agrees to teach on Saturdays. It's not like I have anything else to do. Today I'll be teaching a group of ten-year-olds who've had the misfortune of being born to ambitious parents.

"Saturday is shell day," a little girl says to me cryptically before taking some shells out of her bag.

I've never taught this group before so I have no idea why "Saturday is shell day." For the rest of the lesson, the shells lie there on the table like a worrying reminder that I probably should have made a bit of an effort to find out what the class had done in previous lessons. But in spite of the shells, the four ten-year-olds are a joy to teach. When they've been corrected once, they never make the same mistake again, whether it's vocabulary, grammar, or syntax—in contrast to my adult students. We play the memory game, read stories about sharks who eat people, and make up our own versions of "The Wheels on the Bus."

"What do your parents do?" I ask.

The children stare at me.

"What *jobs* do they do?" I clarify.

The children look relieved and carry on coloring in pictures of dinosaurs with the felt-tips I brought from home.

"My mother is a doctor," says one boy.

"My dad works as a professor," the shell girl says. "In the university."

"Right," I say, slipping in a small correction. "*At* the university? How interesting."

"At the university," the girl says and goes back to coloring her triceratops purple.

"My dad travels a lot. To Japan. And Singapore. And Hong Kong. I get presents. My mom stays at home," says the next boy.

Of course it's only businessmen, doctors, and other highly educated people who can afford to pay for private lessons here. I turn to the last boy.

"And what do your mother and father do?" I ask.

Dismayed, the boy stares at me.

"They write books," he says at last.

"What are the books about?" I ask.

The boy hides his face behind his hands before crying: "About *love!*"

I try to conceal my smile and change the subject so the boy

can recover. The children's natural curiosity, honesty, and joy make me forget to count the minutes until the lesson finishes, and when it's time for them to go we're all sad. A few seconds later they run out of the room and I know I've already become a distant memory to them.

Since Rebecca is at Jakob's parents' place the whole weekend and Leonore's rehearsing, there's half a Saturday and a whole Sunday still to fill. In my head I've made a schedule of jolly little activities. I walk slowly to the first district and look in the windows of the exclusive boutiques. I count the number of women wearing real fur coats on Kohlmarkt (four). On Graben, the wide pedestrian street, I see three young women doing market research for Samsonite. I slow my pace and peer into the Persian rug shop alongside them. When one of the women asks if I would be interested in answering some questions, I feign surprise, then nod and grin.

"Do you own a suitcase with wheels?" the woman asks in German.

"Yes, I do," I reply.

The woman puts a little cross by one of the rows on her sheet of paper.

"Do you own more than one suitcase with wheels?"

"No, I don't."

"Do you know the brand of the suitcase you own?" asks the woman.

"No, sorry," I reply and smile widely.

I love taking part in market-research surveys. And filling out questionnaires. The knowledge that my life can be divided up into simple categories relating to how much I earn, what kind of place I live in, and how many foreign vacations I take a year gives me a sense of security and satisfaction. The fact that there are no gray zones, that everything really can be broken down into black and white. Once, after I'd had a particularly difficult student at Berlitz, I went into the nearest bank and filled in a withdrawal slip just to calm myself down.

"Thank you very much," says the woman. "Have a nice day."

"Was that all?" I say, trying to hide the desperation in my voice.

But the girl has already approached another couple.

I go to one of the few cinemas in Vienna that shows films in their original language. The film doesn't start for another hour and a half so I read Hemingway's *A Moveable Feast* in the foyer and realize I'm in the wrong European city for becoming an author. I should immediately move to Paris, drink cheap red wine, and spend all my time wandering around hungry. After the film I rent a DVD on the way home, and buy some food.

On Sunday I try to sleep in, but fail. Instead, Optimus and I lie in bed and stare at one another. I go to a Kokoschka exhibition in the Museum Quarter and then to the cinema again. I eat dinner at McDonald's and hope none of my students will see me. I make a constant effort not to look at the time to see how many hours I have to endure before I can go to bed and begin my working week again.

While I'm eating my Big Mac I start thinking about how I ought to write a historical novel set in England. It would be about a young orphan girl who becomes a governess at a big spooky mansion. Slowly, she and the dour master of the house fall in love, but there's a big twist: the master's wife is still alive—locked up because she's batshit crazy. Locked in the attic! Once again, the hair on my arms stands on end when I think what an incredible story it's going to be.

6

Fuck you, Charlotte Brontë.

~

I pour sugar into my coffee cup a little too fast and some lands on the table.

"Oops," Stephan says, smiling.

I brush the sugar off the little round metal table and smile back. You should always smile on a date. And be sexy. And fun. I try to think of something fun and sexy to say about sugar but my head's empty. *Brown sugar—like sensual little sun-kissed grains of sand—hahaha!* This is the first date I've been on since the one almost a year ago, when I went out with a doctor who I never heard from again.

"I'm so sick of the warm weather," Stephan says, nodding at the blue sky outside. His accent is so strong it sounds like "ze wuarm wezzer."

The café is in one of the museum galleries and it's pleasantly cool. Around us, the muted voices of the other customers can be heard. Outside it's so warm that the pavement on the streets has turned soft and the air is vibrating. Over the last week, two of the horses and one of the drivers of the coaches that always stand in front of the Hofburg have collapsed from the heat. One of the horses even died.

"Me too," I say. On a date you should always agree with the other person. If you don't, you should come up with charming-yet-convincing counter-arguments that show you are independent but not—God forbid—dogmatic.

"The whole of Vienna gets so dusty and suffocating," Stephan continues. "You can't breathe."

"A bit like . . . a gas chamber," I mumble as I realize my cultural faux pas halfway through the sentence. With Austrians you are, after all, only two generations from some pretty terror-inducing events.

The man sitting in front of me is a prince. Not symbolically, and definitely not in terms of appearance: Stephan really is a prince. Even though the Austrian aristocracy was officially abolished after the First World War, Austrians have continued to use their titles as if to show how meaningless the rest of the world's opinions are to them. Stephan is descended from the house of Deyn-Hofmannstein, and his family owns a castle in Steiermark. We started talking to one another when Leonore and I were at Loos Bar last weekend, and after three days I rang him even though I only had a vague, alcohol-blurred memory of him. But because I'd typed "Prince Stepfam! PIRNC!!!" and his number in my phone, I saw it as a sign I should make a little more effort with my love life.

It was my idea to meet at 11 a.m. at the Natural History Museum to show how alternative and spontaneous I am, rather than in the evening at some bar. But now I'm regretting my decision and wishing this coffee in front of me were something alcoholic and that it was quarter to twelve at night rather than in the morning. So far, our date hasn't been the slightest bit alternative and spontaneous, just clumsy and uncomfortable. The Natural History Museum is normally one of my favorite places, but with Stephan at my side, suddenly everything looks both old and childish. He's shown most interest in the meteorite room, while I mostly wanted to look at the enormous coelacanth and the crocodiles on the second floor.

Now we're sitting in the café, trying not to let our legs touch under the table. Stephan is tall and white blond, but his head is too large and too oblong. Every time I look at him I think of those stone statues on Easter Island. He's wearing light-blue jeans, a pink Tyrolean shirt, and a non-ironic *Janker*, the jacket people wear with lederhosen.

"What do you do? In the day I mean?" I ask.

To show how cool I am, I'm not planning on making any reference to the fact that he's a prince.

"Mostly I deal with the administrative side of our place in Steiermark," Stephan says. "But I try to get to Vienna as often as I can."

"Is the . . . the place open to the public?"

"Yup, that's our primary source of income these days," Stephan says. "We organize conferences, weddings, and parties there. There's a lot to be done. And what do you do?"

Up to now, the tone of our date has been similar to the one I generally have with my students during their first lesson. A dialogue consisting of a question, an answer, question, answer, question, answer. Although Stephan has shown a polite interest throughout, it's as though we have a pane of glass between us.

"I teach English at Berlitz," I reply. "At the moment I'm doing a lot of 'out of house.'"

"What's that?" Stephan asks.

"It means I don't teach at the school. Instead I go out to various companies and teach at their offices. All over Vienna."

"Sounds exciting," says Stephan.

"Well, not really," I say. "And sometimes I feel a bit like a call girl. Though I'm selling English instead of sex."

"There's nothing wrong with prostitutes," says Stephan. "I go to brothels a lot."

Because I'm alternative and spontaneous—*The Natural History Museum! Crrrrrrazy or what?!*—I pretend this doesn't shock me.

"Oh right," I say. "Are there lots of brothels in Vienna?"

Stephan nods. "I'd imagine there are at least twenty," he says. "But I never go to the ones the *Tschuschen* or the Turks go to. Just the classy ones."

Tschusch is racist Austrian slang for people from the Balkans. Once, an AMS student asked me if I knew what a *Tschuschen* handbag was. When I shook my head—already slightly panic-stricken about what his reply would be—he said it was a shopping bag from the supermarket. The same student complained angrily in another lesson about there being "too many turkeys in Austria."

"Oh," I say, staring at Stephan. For some perverse reason I find it kind of arousing that he goes to brothels. I wonder briefly if I should sleep with him just for the experience of having sex with someone who goes to brothels, but the sight of Prince Stephan makes me feel as aroused as a bit of sandpaper. I already know we won't be meeting again.

"I'm a regular at one place," he goes on. "Sometimes I even get a discount there."

Stephan sips his coffee as nonchalantly as if we were still talking about the weather.

"And what kind of discount do you get at a brothel?" I ask. "Do you get two for the price of one?"

Stephan nods. "It's a bit like that. They have one girl who can suck you off for forty-five minutes. I see her a lot."

"Wow," I say. "Forty-five minutes? That's, wow, that's a really long time. I didn't even realize you could suck someone off for that long. Amazing she doesn't get a cramp."

My lessons are forty-five minutes long, I think, *and sometimes I can hardly handle that.*

Stephan takes another sip of his coffee.

"So you go to brothels even if you're in a relationship?" I ask.

"It has happened," Stephan says. "But now my mother wants me to think about settling down."

"So you're looking for a princess for your kingdom? Do the girls have to undergo some kind of challenge first? Like catching a dragon's tail? Or is it the princess who can give the longest blow job that wins?"

Stephan looks at me without saying anything. Since this date has now unmistakably died, I don't have to be charming any more. Instead I roll a few grains of sugar between my fingers and wish I was at home with Optimus and my books. I don't want to be with men like Stephan Deyn-Hofmannstein. Actually, I don't want to be dating. I don't want to pretend. I'm OK with being alone. I like my life. I like my quiet flat, clean kitchen, and my shelves full of books. I like the fact that everything's just where I left it. I don't need anything more, and my solitude makes me neither unhappy nor pathetic.

Despite this, when we've finished our coffee we go on to a temporary exhibition about Chernobyl on the ground floor and look at pictures of kids with missing limbs dressed in knitted sweaters.

~

Outside the museum we stand on the stone steps and compete to be first to come up with an excuse to end the date. It's Stephan who wins.

"Unfortunately I've promised to meet a friend," he says, making a vague gesture towards the center of town.

"Of course," I say. "No problem."

We continue to stand facing one another.

"What are your plans for this afternoon?" he asks, already looking away longingly.

"Oh, same old, same old I guess," I say. "Relaxing at home and masturbating while I listen to a bit of Michael Bublé."

Stephan looks at me. His eyes have become tinged with fear.

"Just joking," I say quickly. "I hate Michael Bublé."

He still doesn't say anything.

"Though I do have a friend who's in a backing choir," I continue. "And she's worked with him and says he's actually very nice. Not at all diva-ish or arrogant. Though you might think he was, judging from his appearance. He looks so smug."

My Michael Bublé knowledge falls on deaf ears. Stephan and I kiss each other on the cheek and go our separate ways without any promises to stay in touch.

Because I can't go to the first district in case I bump into Stephan again, I head to Haydn, the English language cinema in the sixth district. It's only three o'clock and the place is nearly empty. When the trailers start, I try to be happy and relieved at being on my own again and give myself a pat on the back for escaping the fate of becoming the princess who is forced to give Easter-Island-Head forty-five-minute blow jobs. But I don't really feel it. Just emptiness mixed with gnawing dissatisfaction. And it's not until I get home that I realize a bit of popcorn has somehow lodged itself in my hair.

1

I start working so much that my life consists of nothing but my apartment, Berlitz, and the various companies I'm sent to: EON, Strabag, Creditanstalt, Tele2Mobil, Andritz, Wien Energie, BAWAG, Polytec Holding, and a small but enthusiastic sweater-clad group of curators at mumok, the modern art museum. I find pleasure in the tiredness I feel at the end of the day as I haul my bag up the stairs. My bag contains nothing but photocopies on how to write emails correctly in English, because that's all the companies are interested in. If I've taught them well I sometimes manage to get my corporate students' emails to go from sounding frighteningly militaristic—"You send now the invoice!"—to a smidgen less frighteningly militaristic. A major part of the lessons is spent trying to explain the importance of being indirect when speaking English. My students look at me then with a mixture of incomprehension and mild nausea at the idea that anyone would choose a roundabout route when they could just take the Autobahn.

"Good morning," I say to the receptionist at the language school, who looks like he's twelve years old.

"Good morning," he replies.

I find the folder with my name which contains all the day's information cards. A few students are already hanging out by the water cooler and laughter can be heard from the staff-room. While I look through the day's schedule, I notice with irritation that two periods are empty in the middle of the day. I prefer to teach all day long with no breaks.

"There were no students for me at eleven o'clock?" I ask.

"Sorry," the receptionist shakes his head.

It suddenly occurs to me what I should do during that time.

"It's OK," I say, and grin.

At eleven, when my lesson finishes, I hurry over to the optician in the sixth that I'd passed a few days previously. To my relief the sign saying "free hearing test" is still there. When I step into the shop a little bell rings. Everything in the shop is white apart from the hundreds of pairs of glasses and sunglasses displayed on round panels. A woman who's about twenty and wearing stop sign–red lipstick comes out from a room in the back. Her hair is in a tight bun and she's wearing a white coat, just like a doctor.

"How may I help you?" she asks.

"Do you really offer hearing tests?"

"Absolutely," the woman says. "We sell hearing aids too."

"Then I'd like to have a hearing test, please," I reply.

At first the woman (Frau Ruthofer, I see now from her name badge) doesn't move.

"Of course," she says finally. "Would you like to do it now or book an appointment?"

"Now would be perfect," I say. "If it suits you?"

The woman goes to the door while I sneak a look at a pair of Bulgari sunglasses which cost 402 euros. I quickly calculate that I'd need to teach about thirty lessons to buy them.

"My colleague is at lunch right now," Frau Ruthofer explains as she locks the door to the shop. "Come with me."

A minute later, I'm sitting behind a desk in a little sound-proofed room with dark brown walls full of millions of tiny holes. On the floor there's a thick, light-brown carpet and in front of me there's a glass wall. Frau Ruthofer is sitting on the other side. She leans forward and speaks into the microphone.

"The tonal audiometry will consist of ten test sequences per ear. Are you ready?"

"Sorry?" I say.

"The tonal audiometry will . . ."

I shake my head. "I was just joking. You can begin."

For the next ten minutes I sit there, pressing a button whenever I hear various sounds in my left or right ear. I have butterflies in my stomach; it's been a long time since I've felt this happy. Instead of filling out a questionnaire, it's now my body and my hearing that are being tested and categorized. Still, the whole time I feel like Frau Ruthofer is watching me suspiciously and her expression seems to darken with every minute that passes. I worry that it might be because my hearing is so dire.

"Well, that's it, we're finished," Frau Ruthofer says.

Disappointed, I stand up and we go out into the shop again. Frau Ruthofer fetches a few sheets of paper from a printer in the back room.

"Here is your audiogram," she says, peering at the paper.

"This contains your results, what types of sound you were able to detect and at which decibels."

With curiosity I wait for her to continue. Frau Ruthofer finishes the report before putting it down, slightly frustrated.

"Can I ask you something?" she says, in a tone that borders on sharp.

"Of course," I reply.

"Do you ever suffer from tinnitus?" she asks.

I shake my head.

"Middle ear infection?"

Again I shake my head.

"Noise damage? Otosclerosis? Ménière's disease?"

I shake my head for a third time.

"Does anyone in your family suffer from any hearing problems that you're worried may be hereditary?"

"No," I reply, my voice faltering. "They all have good hearing."

"Do you have any kind of hearing problems at all?" Frau Ruthofer almost barks.

"No," I say wretchedly.

"So why did you come here?" Frau Ruthofer exclaims. "Normally it's older—*much* older—people who take this hearing test."

At first I don't answer.

"It was free and I had nothing to do," I admit at last.

Frau Ruthofer says nothing. Then she gives me the papers.

"Congratulations," she says. "You have exceptionally good hearing. Particularly in your left ear."

"Do I?" I cry.

"The details are in the report."

I take it and try to make sense of the figures and the small diagrams, as I process my newly-discovered talent.

Behind me I hear someone knock on the door. Frau Ruthofer unlocks it, and in comes a somewhat older woman, who is also wearing a white coat under her jacket. In her hand she's holding a paper bag from Anker, the sandwich shop, and a Pago apple juice. Angrily, Frau Ruthofer starts telling her colleague that I've just had a hearing test because I had nothing else to do. As though I wasn't standing two meters away from them. With super-hearing.

When I say goodbye and leave the shop, neither of the women replies, but with my new superpower I'm oblivious to their anger.

8

Berlitz has given me a prestigious teaching job. I'm going to teach English to none other than the director of Bank Austria, the country's biggest bank. Because he's a very busy man, the only time he's available is seven in the evening. The fact that Herr Direktor Kolbinger is a very busy man is something that has been impressed upon me three times. The third time, I was this close to pointing out that it wasn't me asking to disturb him.

So now I'm sitting on a bench on Karlsplatz, waiting for seven o'clock to arrive. Right behind me is Bank Austria's marble-clad entrance. The evening is mild and tourists mill about in front of me, looking at the opera house or one of the half-dozen concert-ticket sellers dressed as Mozart in cheap wigs. Large posters announce that the opera will be performing *The Magic Flute* tonight.

Someone sits beside me on the bench. I continue watching a group of Japanese tourists who cover their mouths, titter, and hurry away when one of the ticket sellers says hello to them. The bottoms of one of the Mozart's dark-red velvet trousers are held together with safety pins.

"What's the time?" a voice says beside me in English.

I look at the clock that's right in front of us.

"Ten to seven," I say, and dart a look at the person.

He's big. His hair, clothes, beard, and, most of all, his eyes are big. He might even have the biggest eyes I've ever seen. They're dark brown, just like his hair and his beard would probably be if they weren't so dusty and dry. I turn back to the clock. At the same time I realize the person beside me on the bench is about to ask me something else.

"What's your name?" he asks after exactly thirty seconds.

"Julia."

Now I see he's holding a ratty laptop bag in his hands. His nails are filthy and his fingertips are a dirty yellow.

"Are you from here?" he asks.

Once again I look at the enormous man—no, the enormous *homeless* man—beside me and wonder when he's going to ask me for money.

"No, from Sweden."

"Oh thank the lord, so you're not an Austrian," he says, breathing a sigh of relief.

His comment makes me laugh out loud, which in turn produces a big grin from him, and he leans closer to me.

"I didn't mean that," he said. "Austrians are just a bit weird."

"Weird how?" I ask.

He scratches his beard and ponders.

"Aloof in some way, like they have some big secret in common. One that everyone knows, but that everyone keeps their mouths shut about."

"Maybe that they've got someone hidden in the cellar," I suggest.

The homeless guy nods furiously. "Exactly! And they all seem to be in really bad moods the whole time. On the other hand, they did give the world Arnold Schwarzenegger," he says. "So I'm ready to forgive them."

From the clock I see it's five to seven. I ought to go in to see Herr Direktor Kolbinger.

"Do you really love Schwarzenegger that much?" I ask.

The man turns towards me and makes his eyes hard.

"You're a funny guy, Sully. I like you. That's why I'm going to kill you last," he says in an uncanny imitation of Arnie.

I can't help smiling as I stand up. "Well, have fun," I say.

The homeless guy stands up too. He towers over me, at least a full head taller. "Do you have to go?"

I nod. I know I should make my way to the bank but there's something keeping me here. Now it's three minutes to seven and I'm definitely going to be late for my first lesson with Herr Direktor Kolbinger.

"Bye b—" I begin.

The guy points at the bench.

"Saturday, seven o'clock, same bench," he says. Then he turns and disappears among the crowds.

9

Herr Direktor Kolbinger has the whitest hair I've ever seen and smells of strong, spicy eau de cologne. But aside from those details, our lesson is a little hazy because I can't stop thinking about my encounter with the homeless man. Also, the bank director keeps answering his phone, meaning that we're constantly being interrupted. When the forty-five minutes are over, he tells me his secretary will be in touch to arrange the next lesson. He shakes my hand and almost pushes me out of the room.

When I come out onto Karlsplatz again, I keep an eye out in case the big hairy man has come back. When I fail to see him, I walk all the way home instead of taking Tram 1 and then Bus 48A. Past the Butterfly House, the Natural History Museum, and the Volkstheater. Outside the museum quarter they've already started selling potato wedges and those chestnuts that always smell better than they taste. On the trees, some of the leaves have turned from green to shriveled yellow. I think about the homeless guy's last words and feel slightly annoyed that they sounded like an order.

The next evening I meet Leonore. For the best part of an

hour I let her talk about the argument she had with the Beige Man after he caught her red-handed drinking Coca-Cola rather than Red Bull Cola. The whole time I wonder whether I should mention the man I met. In the end I decide to go for it.

"A homeless guy started talking to me yesterday," I begin. "While I was sitting outside the opera house."

Leonore grimaces. "Ugh," she says. "I hate it when they do that."

"No, he was different," I say. "Quite funny, actually. And kind of sexy in an odd way."

"What did you talk about?"

I immediately regret mentioning it.

"Schwarzenegger."

Leonore looks at me as though I've just let rip a huge fart in the middle of the Opera Ball.

"Men are so pathetic," she mutters.

"He asked if we could meet again," I say. It's not exactly a lie. "On Saturday."

"Oh good God, you didn't say yes, did you?" Leonore exclaims, and for the first time I get the feeling she's actually looking at me.

I don't answer.

"So how long were you talking?" Leonore asks.

"Seven minutes exactly," I reply.

Rebecca's more curious. We're sitting at Café Central, waiting for our cakes to arrive. It's part of our plan to work our way through every famous café in Vienna. We pretend we're there to surround ourselves with cultural history, but really it's just an excuse to stuff ourselves with baked goods.

"Was he English?" Rebecca asks.

"Nah," I say. "He sounded more American."

"What was his name?"

"I didn't ask."

We watch a family with two teenage children sit down at the next table. The tail-coated waiter gives them each a leather-trimmed menu.

"Wonder how he ended up on the street," she says.

"*I* wonder what he's doing in Vienna," I say. "It's hardly the most welcoming place for people like him."

The police recently carried out a major purge of all the homeless people on Schwedenplatz, and they vanished in one night. There was a rumor they'd been shipped off to a little village by the Hungarian border. Lobotomy, forced sterilization, and the slaughterhouse had also been mentioned.

The waiter comes with our order. He places a cherry gâteau in front of Rebecca, while I get a *Himbeer Harmonie*—a half-moon dessert made of raspberry mousse. For a long time neither of us says a word, and all that can be heard is the sound of dessert forks scraping against plates.

"So, are you planning to go?" Rebecca asks finally. "On Saturday?"

"I haven't decided yet," I say.

Actually I've already made the decision to meet him again. It's not like I have anything else to do.

10

On Saturday I'm sitting on the same bench at seven o'clock.

When an older couple sit beside me I give them an irritated glance and look around impatiently. A noisy group of Italian school kids with identical red and blue backpacks walk by. An elderly lady wearing a mink coat. An overly-affectionate couple with their arms round each other's shoulders. A mother with a little boy who's fallen asleep in his stroller. Three businessmen who aren't saying a word to one another. Two girls taking photos of each other in front of the opera house. A teenage boy running towards the metro station. A tall woman stuffing chunks of baguette into her mouth. A boy carrying a double bass case. Several couples holding hands. But no big hairy guy.

Ten minutes pass. Fifteen. Suddenly I realize how pathetic I am. How desperate. That I'm actually looking forward to a date—or whatever this is—with a tramp. That this is the level I've sunk to and that I was enough of an idiot to actually think he'd come. I try to swallow the lump in my throat and get out my mobile to ring Rebecca. She won't judge me; she'll just say the right things. That he's obviously a dope. That he doesn't know what he's missing. That there are plenty of other fish in the sea. That, in any case, I deserve much, much better (which I obviously do, he is *homeless* after all). But I'm even embarrassed to call Rebecca. Now twenty minutes have passed.

Then I see him. He comes cycling through the crowds on a little kid's bike. When he catches sight of me his face breaks into a smile. Several people turn to stare at the giant bearded cyclist. He stops in front of me and carefully leans the bike against the trash bin by the bench.

"You're late," I say.

"I didn't think you'd come," he says. "It was Kobra who said I should probably just check whether you were here or not. And you are—wow!"

I look at the little bike.

"Is it yours?" I ask.

He nods his shaggy head.

"Yep, I bought it and everything. Paid five euros."

"Did you buy it from a child?"

"No, a man. A very small man," the homeless guy says and starts laughing.

Today I notice more details. He's wearing a dark green, long-sleeved T-shirt, a dirty grey sweater, and jeans with holes in them, and he's using a pale-blue rope as a belt. He's barefoot and his feet are dark brown with dirt. On his hands there are several grazes and the knuckles on his right hand are covered in scabs. It looks as though he's trimmed his beard a little—unlike his hair, which looks even bigger and more matted than last time. And his face really is beautiful under all the facial hair. If Hagrid from the Harry Potter books had been younger and hotter he would have looked like this. But today I also notice that he's emitting a pungent, rancid smell.

"What's your name anyway?" I ask.

"Ben," he replies. "And sorry, but I've forgotten yours."

"Julia," I say. "Are you homeless?"

"Yes," Ben replies. "But I just came from a house we might try to squat in. Kobra and the other punks are still there."

"Are you a punk?"

"Nah, but the first time I came to Vienna I walked past Kobra and we started chatting. Then we shared a bottle of vodka and after that I got introduced to the rest of the gang. He might come with me when I go to Berlin."

"Where do you live now?"

"In a bush in the Stadtpark," he says. "But there's a rumor the police are going to kick us all out soon."

I'm so fascinated by Ben and the circumstances of his life that I can't help but ask more questions.

"How did you end up homeless?"

Ben scratches his beard and looks pensive.

"I'm not really. I was just traveling around Europe and, well, the money ran out." He laughs again. As if everything— including him and me and life—is just one big joke.

"Where are you from? Originally?"

"Canada," he replies. "You been there?"

I shake my head. "No. But I've always wanted to go."

"Oh you have to! There's no culture there, of course. Not like here. But the mountains! And the air! Standing on Wreck Beach and just breathing that fresh mountain air. Or driving the pick-up to Bouleau Lake to go fishing. *Man*, I miss Canada!"

His boyish enthusiasm is such a contrast to his almost frightening size that I have to smile.

11

As we talk we're walking along Ringstrasse, which circles the first district. At some point we buy ourselves hot dogs from an Imbiss kiosk and a bottle of red wine from Billa. I pay for the wine and Ben pays for the hot dogs with a heap of change he digs out of his jeans pocket. The drunks that hang out in front of the Imbiss kiosk watch with interest as Ben counts out the coins on the metal counter. When it turns out he has enough they look relieved and almost pat him on the back.

"How old are you?" I ask before taking a bite of my hot dog.

"Twenty-four," Ben replies.

"What?" I turn towards him.

"Twenty-four," he replies.

"A-are you sure?" I stammer. "I thought you were older."

"Beard," he says, pointing at it. "You?"

"I'm almost thi . . . Twenty-nine," I reply.

Ben doesn't just sleep in a bush, he's also a bearded child.

"How tall are you?" I ask.

"Six foot five," he replies. "I think that's about one hundred and ninety-five centimeters."

"So tell me again how you became homeless," I say. "I just don't get *how* people end up that way. I mean, I get why some people do, but not people like you."

Ben doesn't say anything at first.

"It's simple," he says after a while. "What could be easier than just sleeping wherever you want? You see a bit of grass and you sleep there."

"But what about winter?"

"I find an empty house."

"But don't you get scared?"

"Of what?" he says, smiling. "That someone's going to take my smelly old sweater?"

"But is this how you want to live your life?" I ask.

"Why not?" Ben says, shrugging. "I've got nothing to complain about, but I can tell you one thing. The best country to be homeless in is Switzerland. When me and The English were in Geneva, I ate three fantastic meals a day at different hostels."

From what I can make out, The English is some crazy Scot who Ben met in Spain and who came with him to France and Switzerland. In Geneva, Ben and The English realized they'd had enough of each other and went their separate ways in that pragmatic way only men seem to be capable of.

"But how can you afford to travel from one country to the next?"

Ben sticks out his thumb. "I hitch," he says. "Of course, sometimes you just end up walking through industrial park after industrial park, or some seedy residential district, and it's hot as fuck and not a single car passes. And then I earn money by singing badly or telling jokes on the street."

"Can you really make money that way?" I ask.

"Of course I can," he smiles. "The English and I had this whole routine we used to do that people loved. But one time this guy put some money in our box when we were just sitting there taking a break so I ran after him and gave it back. I'm no beggar."

"But do you like sleeping in a bush?" I ask, because I still can't get over his homelessness.

"My bush is totally cool!" he says. "There's space for two and you can't see in from the outside."

"But a *bush*? Wouldn't you rather sleep in a room? On a mattress?"

Ben scratches his beard. I take a last glug from the wine bottle before throwing it away.

"Sure . . . sometimes . . ." he begins. "Especially now that it's started getting colder again in the evenings. That's why I gotta find a house soon."

Suddenly he takes my hand and we walk on. His hand is so large it almost swallows mine and I notice that my heart is beating faster and faster. Under all the dirt, Ben really is one of the most beautiful men I've ever met, with an astounding—and surprising—sense of self-confidence, pride, and joyfulness. Being so close to him sends hot pulses through my body and suddenly I realize I want to kiss him. In fact, I want to have sex with him. My only dilemma is that the stench of him almost makes me retch.

"Why don't you have any shoes?" I ask. "Doesn't it hurt to walk barefoot all the time?"

"When I was in Spain I realized I had holes in my shoes," Ben says. "First I wound a load of duct tape around them but it was impossible to fix them so I threw them into the sea. Unfortunately I realized too late that you can't buy size 47 shoes in Spain because all the Spaniards are like five feet tall. So I had to go barefoot. And in France they're not much taller, and by the time I got to Switzerland I was used to going barefoot. But you should see the calluses under my feet. They're crazy. Want to check them out?"

"No, thank you," I say.

"What do you do then?" Ben asks.

"I teach English at Berlitz," I reply. "Actually I want to be a writer, but sadly it seems all the stories I come up with have already been written. My subconscious memory for plotlines seems to be a lot better than my imagination. Yesterday I had a really good idea for a story about an enormous great white shark that terrorizes a little coastal town. I was so excited about it until I realized it's the plot of *Jaws*."

"You'll be an author one day," he says. "Sometimes things just take a little time."

"I wish I could be so sure of that," I say.

"Maybe you should write something about your own life?" he suggests.

"The life of an English teacher isn't that exciting, unfortunately," I say. "Although I once had a student who only ate things that were white, like rice and yogurt. That was quite weird. And once she asked why we needed the past progressive tense, which is almost an existential question. And another student refused to have me as a teacher because I'd said that every time he said "informations" a puppy died, and every time he said "peoples" a kitten died. He turned out to be a real animal lover."

"How did you end up in Vienna?" he asks.

"Ah, it was . . . a guy," I mumble. "Matthias. He's from around here."

"I hate him already," Ben says.

"When we split up I just stayed here. I've lived in Vienna for almost five years, and now I share my life with Optimus."

On our right we pass the Hofburg for the second, or maybe third, time. From the big clock I see that Ben and I have been walking for almost three hours. Ben seems to be brooding about something.

"So how long have you been with this Optimus?" he asks finally.

"Just a few weeks, but I've got a feeling he wants to break it off. He's started clawing the sofa pretty passive-aggressively."

Ben looks relieved.

"He's a cat!" he cries. "When you said Optimus I thought you might be living with some Hells Angels guy. They have weird names like that sometimes. Like The Axe. Or Apache. I could already see myself being forced to give him a good beating."

He grips my hand even harder.

"Nah," I reply. "My Hells Angels boyfriend won't be out until 2028. You know, they're pretty harsh on triple murderers."

Suddenly Ben stops short. He stands in front of me and takes my face in his hands. Even though I'm not short myself, I have to stand on tiptoe to be able to kiss him. But the second before we kiss each other I'm forced to turn my head away and take a step back because the stench surrounding him is quite simply unbearable.

"Was that too soon?" Ben asks uncertainly.

I nod. "You haven't asked my Sicilian relations for permission yet," I say. "No, seriously though, can you take a shower and wash your clothes somewhere if we see each other again?"

"Oh no, do I smell?"

I nod, and Ben howls with laughter.

"And you don't think it's sexy and manly?"

I shake my head. "And I should be heading home," I say.

"No," he pleads, taking my hand.

"Yes."

I don't tell him my feet have started to hurt. Aside from that, I've had a lot more fun during my hours with Ben than I could have ever imagined, and this surprising fact is something I'm now going to have to go home and think over.

"You don't want to come back to my bush?" he asks with a winning smile. "I put some pieces of cardboard down on the ground."

"Cardboard?" I say.

"And a tarp I lifted from a restaurant."

"Cardboard flooring *and* a tarp?" I shake my head. "I must be crazy saying no to an offer like that but it'll have to be some other time. And you should go back to Karlsplatz and get your little bike before someone steals it."

Ben takes my other hand. "What are you doing tomorrow?" he asks. "Can we meet then?"

"I've got something to do," I say.

He looks disappointed. "Don't you have any time at all tomorrow?" he asks. "Please, please, please?"

"Sorry," I say and shake my head.

"Then I'll just have to kidnap you," Ben says, suddenly tackling me.

He lifts me up and starts running down the street with me

over his shoulder, laughing. I kick him as hard as I can and beat him with my arms until he finally puts me down again. I can feel how red my whole face has turned and how hard my heart is hammering.

"Stop it!" I say, pushing him away. "There's not a girl alive who likes being picked up! And if there is one, she's a prima ballerina at the Kirov ballet, and probably weighs a quarter of what I do. *Never* do that again!"

Ben stops laughing and looks at me. "What do you like then?" he asks.

"Walking side by side," I say. "Like equals."

We've both got our breath back, although my heart's still beating faster than normal.

"OK. Sorry," he says, smiling. "What time do you finish teaching on Monday then?"

"Five."

"And it's Berlitz on Mariahilferstrasse? That big shopping street?"

I nod.

"Then I'll be there," he says.

"It's probably easier if we meet outside the Starbucks that's a bit further down the street. The one on the corner," I say quickly. "That's a better meeting place."

"OK," Ben says.

Once again he leans in to kiss me. I pinch my nostrils and lean forward, my lips in a pout. But at the last moment a wave of *eau de Clochard* hits me—a rich, fruity blend of sweat and garbage—and I have to pull my head away.

"Sorry. I just can't do it."

"OK," Ben says. "I promise not to stink next time."

"Good," I say, and smile.

When I've walked twenty meters I hear Ben shout after me. A man with a hat, whose little dog is doing its business nearby, turns around too.

"We're going to get married and have children!" Ben shouts.

I stare at the towering figure, who I can now only see in silhouette.

"Just so you know!" he continues.

Then he turns and starts walking in the opposite direction. The man in the hat mutters something in German before bending down with a plastic bag pulled over his hand. I gaze after the stinking twenty-four-year-old with the filthy feet and wonder if we'll ever see each other again.

12

The next day is a Sunday. My bed is right by the window, so I sit wrapped up in my covers looking out onto the courtyard with its enormous oak. Apart from an old woman airing her sheets on the third floor of the apartment building on the left, there's no one around, so I carry on staring at the tree. I think about Ben and wonder why I told him I didn't have time to meet him today. In the end, I call Rebecca to find out what she's up to. And what I'm up to.

"I'm just on my way to Heldenplatz," she says. "Jakob's running a marathon."

Several voices can be heard around her.

"I didn't know Jakob was a runner," I say.

"He's just started, because he's worried about getting old." A vuvuzela blows somewhere near her. "Yesterday he ran five kilometers."

"Oh well that's OK then," I say. "Everyone says that once you've got those first five kilometers out of the way, the next thirty-seven are nothing."

"Wait, someone's on the other line," Rebecca says suddenly.

After a minute she calls back.

"Jakob collapsed 200 meters from the starting line," she says, out of breath. "I have to go to UNO City as quickly as possible to pick him up."

"Is he OK?" I ask.

"Apparently he got really dizzy and they've said he can't go on."

"His skinny little Jesus-legs just aren't made for marathons, only for building violins," I say. "Do you want me to come along? You can pretend to be Mary and I'll be Mary Magdalene."

"No, it's OK. And that would mean I was having sex with my own son—bleurgh," Rebecca says. "See you at Berlitz."

"OK," I say. "I hope Jakob's all right."

For a second I contemplate calling Leonore, but seeing as we actually only use each other to have someone to go out with and don't even really like each other that much, I forget that idea. I look around the flat and suddenly hate my solitary life, and myself for choosing it. I jump up, pull down all the books from the shelves and give myself the triple challenge of putting them back in size, color, and chronological order. After an hour and a half of careful coordination I get a kick out of seeing Kate Atkinson's *Started Early, Took My Dog* fitting in perfectly beside Cormac McCarthy's *No Country for Old Men*, Ian McEwan's *Atonement* beside Paul Scott's *The Jewel in the Crown*, and so on.

When all the books are in place, I sit on the sofa and stare at them. Optimus jumps up and lies down next to me. I start rubbing his tummy until the cuddles turn into a play-fight. Optimus opens his eyes wide in surprise between bouts, licking my arm, clawing it, and biting it in turn. When he finally runs off I notice that my forearm is so scratched that it's bleeding in several places and there are a number of blood-stains on the sofa.

"I know you do it because you love me," I say to Optimus, who has jumped up on the windowsill and is licking his back frenetically.

I carry on looking at my bloody arm and decide to start a relationship with Ben. I will have the courage to change my life, experience new things, and, just for once, take the path less traveled. Or in this case, the man less washed. I deserve a little sex, even love. And Ben's going to Berlin soon anyway.

13

Standing by the whiteboard, I suddenly can't remember how to spell "house." I send small SOS calls to my internal English dictionary but hear nothing but an empty, unanswered echo. In panic, I stare at the words I've already written on the board:

ANNA LIVES IN A BIG

Bettina, Steffi, and Hans look at me. From the next room I hear Claire and her students laughing at something. The green marker hovers a couple of centimeters from the white-board while I stand glued to the spot. *Haus? Huoz? Oh Anna, you everywoman, where do you live?* In a flash of inspiration I turn to my students.

"Who can spell 'house'?" I exclaim with a smile.

Slowly, Hans puts his hand up and I give him the pen. As he walks up to the board I sit down on one of the chairs and glance over at Bettina and Steffi. Have they noticed how strangely I'm behaving today? That I haven't corrected half the mistakes they've made and that Hans has been free to tell us he is Christ, rather than a Christian, because I've stopped caring? That the whole day is just one long countdown to five o'clock when I can meet Ben again?

"I am afraid of dogs," Steffi reads slowly from the book.

"*Ich bin erfreut von Hunden,*" translates Hans quietly to himself, nodding.

"No, no, it means . . ." I start, but I can't finish, as I'm suddenly struck by the feeling—no, *the knowledge*—that Ben will have forgotten that I said we should meet at Starbucks. He'll be standing there outside Berlitz waiting for me so everyone can see him. When the five-to-five bell rings I'm the first to hurl myself out of the room and I'm close to pushing Bettina out of the way because she's dawdling so much. First I head for the toilet for a pee and then I rush down the stairs. *Please let him not be standing outside Berlitz. Please let him not be standing outside Berlitz. Please let him not be standing outside Berlitz.* When I come out onto Mariahilferstrasse I look around at all the shoppers and immediately catch sight of him. He's leaning against a tree a couple of meters away, smoking. With a tense smile I walk over to him.

"Hi," I say.

"Hi," Ben says. He smiles back and throws away his hand-rolled cigarette.

"Didn't we agree to meet outside Starbucks?" I ask.

"Did we? I thought we were meeting outside Berlitz at five o'clock."

"No," I say.

To my relief he at least doesn't smell, although this could be because the weather is colder today. He's also in different clothes. The jeans are the same, but he's wearing a baggy hoodie that was probably dark blue once upon a time. He's still barefoot.

"I managed to have a shower at a hostel, but not to clean my clothes," Ben says. "But luckily I found some others when I was looking through my closet. I don't think they smell as bad."

Proudly, he does a twirl to show off his new outfit.

"Your closet?" I ask.

"A plastic bag," Ben replies. "I keep it hidden in another bush. It's a miracle no one's stolen it yet. You look very nice today."

"Thanks," I say and look over at the entrance to Berlitz, where Steffi is just coming out. She immediately lights a cigarette and hurries off down the street. A few seconds later, Bettina comes out. She's talking on her mobile and gives me and Ben a curious look as she gets a pack of cigarettes out of her bag.

"I was thinking about you all day yesterday," Ben says with a big grin.

"Come on, let's go," I say quickly.

We walk to the first district and buy loads of food. Then we sit on a bench in the Volksgarten, where almost all the roses have already withered. There's only one rosebush that is still in bloom, with white, crinkly petals. I lay out the food between us. Ben immediately opens one of the Ottakringer beers and downs the whole can.

"Do you drink a lot?" I ask.

For the first time I notice that Ben looks uncomfortable.

"All homeless people drink," he says at last, in a tone that suggests that it's obvious. "Otherwise you can't sleep. The only way to sleep rough every night is to get drunk. Then you don't feel the cold either."

I look at the white roses a bit further off and think how different the worlds we live in are. Ben's, where it's essential to get drunk to survive the night, and mine, where the day's biggest tragedy was that the photocopier in the staffroom was broken and Ken had taken my favorite coffee cup.

"How long have you been sleeping outside?" I ask.

"For about a year," Ben replies, opening another can of beer.

I seem to be the only one interested in the bread, cheese, salami, and olives.

"What did you do before that, then?"

"I drove tow trucks for a while. In Canada, I mean. And worked as a moving man. For a whole summer I picked earthworms for use as live bait."

"Earthworms! I didn't even know that was a job."

Ben nods. "It's a big thing in Canada. Mostly completely illegal because they don't pay fair wages and they get away with it by hiring Pakistanis or Vietnamese or desperate people like me."

"How do you even pick earthworms?"

Ben points at his legs. "You have a bucket tied onto one leg, which you put the worms in, and on the other leg you have a bucket of sand. Then you creep across a field the whole night, hunched over. You have to sand your hands down to get a good grip on the worms and make sure you get the whole worm without it breaking. Sometimes you don't get a single worm, and sometimes you get thousands, particularly during the mating season."

"It sounds awful," I say.

"It was," Ben says. "I've had jobs so shitty I've just wanted to cry sometimes. Like being a moving man, carrying someone's piss-stained mattress for a few measly dollars an hour.

Compared to that, this life seems much better. So, what's the worst job you've had?"

I think about it.

"Most jobs have been pretty terrible because they were so boring," I say. "But once I worked as an assistant for an architect who had lost a bit of his brain. He'd been in a flying accident and had a big dent in his forehead where the brain was missing. That job was awful because it was hard not to stare at his forehead whenever he was talking. So I always stared at the handkerchief in his breast pocket—which might have been the reason I got fired in the end."

"But he was totally normal otherwise?" Ben asks. "Without part of his brain?"

"I think so," I say. "He was just quite nasty sometimes. And all the pencils always had to be super sharp, but perhaps that's some sort of architect thing?"

"I must draw a skyscraper *now*!" Ben shouts. "A sheikh in Dubai wants to have a skyscraper that looks like an enormous cock!"

"No! No! None of the pencils are sharp enough!" I cry. "My career as an architect is *over*!"

"You bitch of an assistant," Ben says. "This is your fault! If I had a forehead I would slap myself on it right now."

We grin at one another.

"Perhaps Berlitz isn't so bad after all," I say. "What do your parents do?"

Ben takes a sip of beer before he answers. "My mum works as a cleaner and my dad was a bricklayer. Then he had problems with his throat so now he just sits around at home and watches TV."

"Do you have any siblings?"

Ben shakes his head. "Just a cousin," he says. "Who died."

"What happened?"

Ben shrugs his shoulders. "He started hanging around with the wrong kind of people in Vancouver and that was the end of that."

We're silent for a while and I think again what different worlds we live in. In mine and Rebecca's circle of friends, "the wrong kind of people" are fully-grown adults who still tell you that they're Team Edward or Team Jacob.

"Tell me about the guys you've met," I say with a smile. "Since you became homeless."

A big grin spreads across Ben's face. "Swiffer! In Amsterdam there was this Albanian who everyone called Swiffer. He was a total addict, of course. But what made Swiffer unique was that he loved cleaning. So people would invite him over and for half a gram of coke he would be up the whole night and clean the entire house in between sniffing lines."

Behind us on Ringstrasse, a tram rings its bell. Ben finally takes a bit of bread and a little cheese and starts to eat.

"Then there was a Serb, Drago—we called him Drago and Gabbana—who only stole designer clothes. He went into shops and hid the clothes under his own and then he sold them. But he wasn't a very nice man. Once he beat up another guy who he thought had looked at him weird. You know, you're really vulnerable when you're homeless. When I was in Geneva, a group of teenagers poured gasoline on some dude and set a match to him just because he was lying asleep on the ground, so now he has no face and is completely blind."

For a long time, neither of us says anything.

"I really know how to seduce a lady, don't I?" Ben says after a while.

"One more story about Albanian cleaners or people getting burned and I'm yours for life," I say, grinning.

"You're actually my first girlfriend," Ben says. "My first and last."

I almost choke on an olive. "You've never had a girlfriend?"

Ben shakes his head. "I have gone out with girls, of course, but I've never seen the point of relationships. Although girls always think I'm going to change my mind if we sleep together. How many boyfriends have you had, then?"

"Quite a few," I say. "Although most of them were idiots, I now realize in hindsight. You've really never had a girlfriend?"

Ben looks at me and shrugs his shoulders.

"I knew that one day I'd know when I'd found The One," he says, taking another piece of bread. "And now I have. I stood watching you for a really long time when you were sitting on that bench in Karlsplatz, and I knew that you would be my wife and the mother of my children."

"You just saw me sitting on the bench and you knew all that?" I ask.

Once again, Ben nods.

"My mum's psychic," he says. "So I probably get it from her. Every time anything bad is around the corner she dreams about dogs, and depending on how they behave she knows what's going to happen. I looked at you and you were so beautiful and I just knew."

Behind us, a tram dings again. My body suddenly feels feverish and my groin is on fire.

"Come on," I say.

14

As soon as we get to my flat we have sex. We almost have it on the hallway floor but I manage to steer Ben into the bedroom. We keep kissing as we tear each other's clothes off. Optimus, who's been lying asleep on the bed, rushes out of the room so fast he loses his footing and slides into the door-frame with a thud.

"You're so fucking sexy," Ben murmurs while he kisses my neck hard.

The sex is wild and full-on and very different from what I've had before. I feel shy and daring all at the same time.

"I'm so crazy about you, you know that?" Ben says afterwards. "You make me feel totally weak and I talked about you so much yesterday that in the end Kobra told me to shut up."

"I've never met anyone like you," I say, truthfully.

Ben gets me in an iron grip and hugs me till it almost hurts.

"Come with me if you want to live," Ben says in my ear with an Austrian accent and a deep voice.

"Arnold again?"

"*Terminator 2.*"

"Are you sure it's not Schwarzenegger you've got a thing for?"

"How could you *not* have a thing for that man?" Ben exclaims in mock surprise. "Have you seen his smile?"

"If you want to take a shower, you're welcome to," I say.

When Ben gets up, I see his naked body in full for the first time. He's thin. It must have been all the layers of clothes that made me think he was heavier and bigger than he actually is. His hips and collarbones jut out in a way they shouldn't, and you can see his ribs. He has no hair on his chest and now I can see too that he doesn't have any tattoos, even though I thought he'd be the type to cover his body with ink. Together, we go into the kitchen.

"There's shampoo, conditioner, and body wash in the shower," I say.

"Do you have any scissors I can trim my beard with?" Ben asks.

"Yes, in the bathroom cabinet," I say.

I hear Ben turn on the shower and start rummaging around among the bottles on the floor.

"I'm going to smell like a little girl," Ben says, laughing.

While he's showering I make some sandwiches and pour us some red wine. Then I throw his clothes in the washing machine and while I wait for him to finish I watch TV and try to coax Optimus out from behind the sofa where he's hiding. I notice that Ben's hip bones have left small bruises on the insides of my thighs. I carefully stroke the small pale-blue marks.

"Is this a laminating machine?" I hear from the kitchen.

Ben comes into the living room. He's wearing my jogging

pants and has a towel wrapped around his shoulders. Water drips from his hair. And he hasn't just cut his beard, he's shaved it off.

"Wow," is the only thing I can say. For the first time, I can really see his face. His lips are bigger and his cheeks more hollow than I thought.

Ben strokes his cheeks a little bashfully. "I feel so naked," he says. "Like a newborn baby."

"Like a pretty sexy newborn baby in that case," I say, but quickly add: "Though not in a pedophile way, of course. A baby like . . . like . . . hmm, well, that didn't quite come out right. You look sexy anyway."

Ben jumps on me and starts nibbling my neck again. His hair drips water on my face. It ends with us having sex again, on the sofa this time.

15

Claire from Berlitz is having a goodbye party in one of the bars in the museum quarter, thereby encapsulating everything I hate about being an adult. The Berlitz gang are sitting awkwardly around three wobbly metal tables, well aware that we're only here out of fear that no one will come to our own goodbye parties.

"To Claire," Dagmar says, lifting her mineral water.

"To Claire," everyone repeats, as we raise our glasses.

Claire lifts her glass too, but doesn't drink. Perhaps it has something to do with the little orange L'Occitane bag by her feet, which contains the present we had popped out to buy that afternoon. The L'Occitane shop is right next to the school.

"Why are you stopping teaching?" asks Randall's young Bulgarian girlfriend, who we're all meeting for the first time. She's also the only one who's not a language teacher, which causes an uncomfortable imbalance in the group, especially since Dagmar turned up.

"I'm going back to school," Claire says. "In London."

"Bloody students," Sarah says in a voice that almost sounds like she's joking.

Everyone laughs politely.

"Thanks, Sarah," Claire says.

Everyone laughs politely again.

"It's going to be so nice to be on the other side again," Claire goes on, stretching. "Just sitting there listening to someone else making all the effort."

"As long as you don't start posting loads of photos of you sleeping till one in the afternoon and stuff," Sarah says.

Again everyone laughs politely.

"What I wouldn't give to be a student again," Randall says.

I try to look at the time discreetly because I'm meant to be meeting Ben in half an hour.

"You're not too old to start studying again," Karen says. "I've got several older students at the university." Karen also teaches at the university. Something I would much rather do than slave away for Berlitz.

"Twenty-seven isn't too old to go to university," Randall's Bulgarian girlfriend says, lovingly brushing a lock of hair from his forehead the way you only do at the beginning of a relationship.

"You're not twenty-seven," Dagmar says. "You're thirty-four. I've seen your papers."

Randall's face turns as red as a beet and he looks both terrified and furious all at once. His Bulgarian girlfriend turns towards him.

"You're thirty-four?" she says, wide-eyed.

"Randall, you liar," I say delightedly. This revelation has made the evening significantly more interesting.

"Why would you lie about how old you are?" Mike asks.

"As if *you* tell the truth about your age when you're looking for acting work," Randall says.

His girlfriend now has a very uncertain smile, and I notice that she's taken her hand from his thigh.

"Did I hear right? Did you just compare your girlfriend to a *job*?" Mike asks.

"How could you lie to your own girlfriend?" Sarah asks.

"Yeah, Randall, explain yourself," I say gleefully.

"Yeah, go on," Mike says.

"OK, can we stop talking about it?" Randall snaps.

Randall's lie is all we talk about until it's time for me to go. I give Claire a hug and wish her good luck with her studies.

Because I don't want anyone to see me with Ben I've agreed to meet him outside the Volkstheater, which is close to the museum quarter and my flat.

When I get there, he's already sitting on the stone steps, eating a *Manner Schnitte*, the popular Austrian wafer-biscuit. It must be the intermission because there are lots of pale people wearing glasses smoking outside the theater. Some are holding champagne flutes. I go up to Ben with a big smile, and we kiss.

"Are you trying to blend in with the Austrians?" I say, gesturing at the *Manner Schnitte* that he's still holding in his hand.

"It's the most disgusting thing I've ever eaten," Ben says and throws the half-eaten wafer away. "And I've eaten dog biscuits."

"Because you were so hungry?" I ask.

"No, in school," he says. "It just seemed like fun."

"I once ate a lot of raspberry yogurt before realizing it was covered in mold," I say.

We kiss again.

"I've been so fucking horny all day just thinking about seeing you again," Ben says and grabs hold of my butt.

"Not in front of Austria's cultural elite," I laugh.

"Julia?" someone says suddenly behind me.

I turn around and see Sarah, who must have left Claire's goodbye drinks just after me. Damn.

"I didn't mean to intrude," she goes on. "I just wanted to see whether it was really you. I didn't realize you . . ." She leaves the rest of the sentence unfinished and looks from me to Ben and back again.

"I'm Ben," Ben says, stretching out his hand. "Sorry, I just grabbed Julia's ass with this."

"Sarah," Sarah replies, ignoring the hand. "I don't think I've seen you before. Do you live in Vienna?"

"Yep," he says. "In a bush in Stadtpark."

"He does *not* live in a bush," I say, as though what he said was a joke.

"Yes I do," Ben says.

"Sometimes," I say quickly. "Just sometimes. In the summer. For the fresh air."

"Why do you do that?" she asks.

"Why not?" Ben shrugs.

"You almost seem proud of it," Sarah says, and I suddenly remember what a bitch she can be.

A bell rings from inside the theater, and the people on the steps throw away their cigarette butts and empty their champagne glasses before going in again. The murmuring around us dies down.

"Why shouldn't I be proud of it?" Ben asks.

"Because it's an odd thing to be proud of," she says.

"Is it?" he snaps.

I get the sense there's going to be a fight soon if I allow this to continue.

"How did you even meet?" Sarah asks.

"It's a long story and we have to go now," I say. "Bye, Sarah!"

I drag Ben off along Neustiftgasse and curse Vienna's little international Berlitz/theater world, which can be suffocatingly incestuous and gossipy sometimes. My secret's out. Sarah shares a flat with Markus, who goes out with Ziggi, who's helping Leonore with the props and costumes for her new play. Sarah will tell Markus everything, and he'll tell Ziggi, who'll tell Leonore, who'll spread the news to the rest of the world. My short, sweet hibernation with Ben is now definitely over.

16

Soon, Ben is waiting for me almost every day after work. After careful instruction he's learned to wait outside Starbucks, even if he no longer looks quite as homeless after shaving off his beard and washing his hair thoroughly a couple of times over at my place. Happy as a little kid, he usually has some plan for what we should do.

"Come on, let's go to the Donauinsel," he says one day when I finish a bit earlier than usual.

"But then we have to take the metro," I say. Ben's financial situation is something we never discuss, so I tend to avoid situations where the issue of money might come up.

"And buy a ticket . . ." I add gently.

"I earned a bit of money today," he says. "I was passing a shop and saw a guy who was about to wash the windows. So I asked him if he needed any help and he was so glad to get out of doing it himself he paid me twenty euros. And it only took a quarter of an hour."

On our way to the long, slender island on the River Danube, Ben starts talking to a guitar-playing Rastafarian and in no time at all they're having a discussion about what it's like to perform on the street in different countries (London = impossible, Barcelona = best money, Amsterdam = best audience). When they part, Ben promises to come to some party the Rastafarian is having in a couple of weeks.

"Stay cool, man," the Rastafarian says.

"You too," Ben says.

"You seem to be able to talk to anyone," I comment when we step off the metro. "So far I've seen you start chatting to at least four different strangers."

"It's just what I do," he says. "I don't even think about it. How would you meet anyone new otherwise?"

We take the steps down. Since it's a warm autumn day, there are lots of other people on the way to and from the island. There's music coming from some nearby bar.

"If a woman did it, people would think she was either crazy or asking to be raped," I say. "Or both."

"No," Ben says.

"Yes, unfortunately that's how it is," I say, nodding.

"No," he repeats. "Why would that be the case?"

"Because . . . because . . . ." I begin. "Because of the reasons I just said. Women can't start talking to complete strangers in the way you do. You can do it because you're a guy and you're tall and you look strong."

"That's not true at all," he says. "I know lots of girls who do it. So how do you meet new people? Do you even ever meet anyone new?"

"I meet new people all the time," I reply.

"Where?"

"At work," I say. "It's really annoying. New people are the worst."

"But that's crazy!" Ben exclaims. "If you think like that you'll just meet the same old people all the time."

"Maybe," I say. "But after a certain age you stop looking for new friends anyway. And if you don't, there's probably something wrong with you."

We find a spot near the water not far from the metro station and sit down. Several of the guys around us have bare chests and two rollerbladers fly by. A bit farther away, a girl throws a pink plastic bone into the water and her golden retriever hurls itself in and fetches it. A young family has spread out a picnic blanket, even if their two children seem more interested in poking something in the grass with sticks.

"I'm going to jump off the bridge," Ben says suddenly.

He leaps up and pulls off his T-shirt. Then he walks quickly to the bridge that stretches across the river, where a walkway runs on a second level under the metro track. I look towards the bridge and realize it must be at least fifteen meters down to the water. Now he's climbing over the railing. A little bunch of Turkish guys who are all wearing white jeans gather around him when they realize he's going to jump. Ben waves at me.

"Hey!" I hear him yell.

I wave back and feel my cheeks redden. Then he jumps, and as he does so he pulls his legs towards his chest and puts his arms round them. With a dull thud he lands in the water and the guys on the bridge clap and wolf whistle. Grinning from ear to ear, with rosy cheeks, Ben swims to the water's edge where I'm sitting. When he gets out of the water he shakes himself like a dog.

"Weren't you scared of doing a belly-flop?" I ask.

He looks at me as though the thought had never occurred to him. "No," he replies. "I did everything right. The only time I got it wrong was when I was drunk and sprained my ankle."

"Maybe I should jump too," I say thoughtfully and look towards the bridge.

"Now that I would never allow," Ben says.

"You'd 'never allow' it? Are you my Victorian governess? Why not?"

"Because you're not ready," he replies. "Or prepared."

"I don't want to jump off the bridge anyway," I say, a little sulkily.

Suddenly I sit up straight and turn to him. "Ben," I say, "I like being organized. I like a life with no surprises. I like paying bills. I love doing jigsaws. One day I'm sure I'll start doing crosswords. After that it's almost inevitable that I'll start going to crossword conventions in the hope of meeting other people who like to solve crosswords and do jigsaws and pay their bills. Because there must be more of us. And I'm looking forward to it. It's not something I'm ashamed of. I know I'm cool. But I don't understand why *you* think I'm cool."

He looks at me. "Because you're beautiful and you have a beautiful heart," he says.

"But you don't know that," I say. "Once I didn't correct a student when she said that she was a vegetable instead of a vegetarian just because I thought it was so funny. So she's probably still going round telling people she's an inanimate piece of plant matter. A kind person wouldn't have done that."

"I do know," Ben says. "I know you have a good heart. You can see that sort of thing. Why do you want to be with me then?"

"Did I have any choice?" I say.

He gives me a strange look.

"I've never met anyone like you before," I continue, and shrug. "And you're always in a good mood."

"*Hell yeah!* You have to be," Ben exclaims cheerfully. "There's so much shit in life that you *have* to focus on the positives. There's always something to be happy about. Even when I was starving and sleeping in a ditch, there was still something to laugh about."

He lies down beside me and closes his eyes while I keep on looking at him and feel something in my chest—a warm, fluttery something—that I haven't felt for many years. In spite of that, I am completely aware that we have no future. He's a twenty-four-year-old tramp with no education. Or shoes. I don't want to have a long-term relationship with, much less marry, someone who works as a moving man or an earthworm picker, and who doesn't have any prospects.

"Why didn't you go to university?" I ask.

"Does it matter?" Ben says a little peevishly, opening his eyes and looking at me.

"No," I lie.

"It really wasn't something my parents cared about," Ben says. "My dad thinks 'real men' work, they don't go to university. My parents never helped me with my homework and when I asked for help my dad just grunted: 'Don't they teach you that in school?' The best way of learning something, according to him, was the rolled-up belt that hung from a nail on the wall."

"But perhaps it's something you should consider," I say. "Going back to school? It's free here and everything."

"Never going to happen," he replies.

I'm surprised by how irritated I feel at Ben's reply but I tell myself it doesn't matter anyway. He'll soon carry on drifting through Europe and I'll return to my old life.

We lie there in silence side by side, enjoying the autumn sun and listening to the gentle murmur of the river, the voices around us, and the music from the bar, which is now playing Haddaway's "What is Love." Ben's hand finds its way to mine and we intertwine our fingers.

"What do you think your people who love paying bills are doing right now?" Ben asks after a while.

"They're still wandering in the desert," I reply.

When it gets dark we take the metro back to my place.

17

eonore has asked to meet me at Café Westend at the end of
Mariahilferstrasse. When I arrive she's already there, which
is the first warning sign. The people in the café are a mix of
young people talking excitedly to one another and hunch-
backed seniors cutting up their schnitzels and boiled potatoes
at a snail's pace. At one of the tables, three men with weather-
beaten faces and fake leather jackets are looking as though
they're having a meeting about stolen Audis. If I didn't know
it was easy to find a parking space nearby, I'd wonder why
Leonore had chosen such a—for her—shabby place.

As soon as Leonore catches sight of me she gets up and we
kiss each other once on the cheek.

"So," she begins. "Have you just come straight from work?"

I nod and hang up my jacket.

"How was it?" Leonore asks.

"Do you really want to know?" I ask and sit down.

Leonore beams and nods. That's the second warning sign.

"I have a student who I'm friends with on Facebook and
LinkedIn for some reason," I begin. "And he's been promoted.

So he updated his LinkedIn details with his new job title. And loads of people liked the new job title. And my student liked the new job title. So I liked his new job title and I liked that my student liked his new job title. But then in class my student didn't like it when I told him that I'd liked that he liked his new job title. So during the break my student unliked his new job title." I shake my head. "Being friends with students is such a minefield. You can't be friends with them. It's a lesson I should have learned by this point. It's like that Christmas Eve football match between the soldiers during the First World War. At some point you always go back to being British or German soldiers trying to kill each other.

"And before that I had two female students from the same company who seemed to hate each other so I ended up having to be a diplomat as well as a teacher.

"And before that I was doing homework tutoring for a fifteen-year-old girl who has a 2,000 euro handbag but still can't use 'could' and 'would' correctly."

I can see that Leonore hasn't listened to a word of my story. Every muscle in her body is poised for the chance to speak.

"How are rehearsals going?" I ask.

Leonore springs to life again like a jack-in-the-box.

"Oh, the actors left the rehearsal room in such a state yesterday that I almost lost it," she replies. "Am I their slave or what? By the way, are you still going out with that homeless guy? I heard about him from Sarah."

I can't help smiling a little. "Leonore, is this some kind of intervention? Shouldn't there be more people here in that case?"

"I just want to make sure you know what you're doing," she says.

"I know what I'm doing," I say.

"That he's not taking advantage of you."

"He's not taking advantage of me."

"That you're not going to get hurt."

"I'm not going to get hurt."

"That it doesn't end with you coming home one day and finding your VCR is gone and you never see him again."

"Well, it's not 1987, so I don't have a VCR," I say. "So if he took anything, it would probably be the DVD player."

"Julia, he's homeless," Leonore says. "What kind of future do you have? Does he have any education? Does he have any employment experience? Does he even want a job? Have you given him any money?"

For the first time I don't answer, because her questions make my muscles stiffen and clench. Suddenly I feel like I'm going to cry, even though I'm getting increasingly angry with Leonore.

"I just want to make sure you've thought this through," Leonore says.

I try to control my voice, so as not to give away my mixture of anger and sadness.

"I'm grateful that you're concerned about me, Leonore, and I really want to reassure you that I know what I'm doing. I have no plans to get involved in a serious relationship or get married to him. Particularly because he's heading off to Berlin soon and then, I assume, back to Canada. At the same time, I'm a grown woman and I feel a bit insulted that I'm having to justify my relationship."

To tell the truth, Ben hasn't mentioned Berlin since our first date and sometimes I almost hope he'll stay in Vienna. Then I have to remind myself that it's just a brief adventure.

"Sarah said he was really aggressive," Leonore says.

"What?" I exclaim. "No, he wasn't."

"Well, she said he behaved extremely aggressively when she asked a couple of simple questions."

"Sarah's an idiot," I say. "If anyone was being aggressive it was her."

"I want you to fall in love and be happy. But this guy really doesn't sound right for you."

My whole body is still rigid and I don't want to make eye contact with Leonore just now. I think about the time she told me that as soon as she quit her job as a consultant for a multinational company in Vienna and stopped having a real career, her and the Beige Man's sex life improved. It's one of the most tragic things I've ever heard.

"We don't need to talk about it right now," Leonore says. "Just think about what I've said. There are more adventurous guys than this homeless man."

"*Adventurous?*" I ask, looking at Leonore.

"Yes," she says. "It's become clear now that that's what you're after. But he's not the only one."

"I'm not after adventurous guys," I say.

"OK, enough," Leonore says.

To my relief we change the subject and talk instead about a mutual friend who's moving to Dubai, about Leonore's plans to renovate her kitchen, about Leonore's latest obsession with raw food, and more about Leonore. Suddenly Leonore waves her hand.

"Gernot!" she calls.

A somberly dressed guy with melancholy eyes walks over to us. I realize immediately what Leonore's up to and wonder what the chances are of her being hospitalized if I pour my *Wiener Melange* over her.

"Come sit down," Leonore tells him, looking delighted. "This is my friend Julia."

Gernot and I shake hands. He's shorter than me and looks as though he can't be more than twenty-two.

"How are you?" Leonore says.

"Not so fine," Gernot replies, shaking his head. "My eyes are hurting again."

A waiter comes over to take his order.

"And I should clean my apartment," Gernot goes on when the waiter disappeared. "But . . . I can't."

The reason Gernot can't clean his apartment remains a mystery.

"Gernot helped me out a bit with my website a couple of years ago," Leonore explains. "That's how we got to know each other."

"That's nice," I say.

Gernot stares grimly ahead of him.

"He works in IT," Leonore says.

"That's nice," I say again.

Suddenly Leonore looks at her phone.

"Oh no!" she cries. "I have to be off. But you should stay. My treat!"

Before either Gernot or I can say anything, Leonore is gone. Thirty seconds later, I get the following text from her:

Gernot almost climbed the Grossglockner. Adventurous!!!

I put my phone away and try to think of something to talk about with Gernot-who-almost-climbed-the-Grossglockner. I'd much rather have gone home, but Gernot already looks as though he has the weight of the world on his shoulders, so I don't have the heart to add to his misery.

"So er . . . Gernot," I begin. "What do you like to do in your spare time?"

Gernot thinks for a moment.

"I like being out in nature," he replies.

I try to come up with a follow-up question.

"And what do you like to do out in nature?"

"Oh, just be out of doors."

We're silent for a few seconds.

"Where do you go when you want to get out into nature?" I ask in the end.

"Around Vienna."

"And . . . do you like cooking?" I ask.

"Sometimes," Gernot answers.

"Whole sentences," I correct him.

"What?"

I feel my cheeks grow hot. "I mean that it's better to reply in whole sentences," I explain. "'Sometimes I like to cook.' That way you learn a language better and more quickly."

Gernot doesn't say anything.

"I work as an English teacher at Berlitz," I say apologetically. "And apparently I've fallen victim to an occupational hazard."

Gernot suddenly brightens up.

"Then maybe you can tell me why people in American films always say 'What's up?'" Gernot says. "What do they mean, 'up'? What is up? Why not down?"

I clear my throat before starting to explain with the most easily-understandable words and the clearest pronunciation I can manage.

"Some people say it's a short way of saying 'What's up with you,' and others think it's a short way of saying 'What's the update,'" I reply. "But it's a silly bit of slang and shouldn't be used, because you can't really give an answer."

Gernot looks disappointed.

"But did you know that the correct answer to 'How do you do?' is 'How do you do?'" I try to console him. "You answer a question with a question. It's quite funny, isn't it? But of course there aren't many people who say that, these days. Except in *Downton Abbey*."

"I've never seen *Downton Abbey*," Gernot says. "It's not my kind of program."

"Me neither," I say. "But I assume they say it on there."

We sit in silence again because we've both realized we have no idea why we're here. I glance at the men in the fake leather jackets and realize I'd rather be sitting with them discussing whether or not we can trust Sergei. In the end I stand up.

"Gernot," I say. "It was really nice meeting you but I have to go now."

"OK," Gernot says, sounding like Eeyore.

After I've left Café Westend and am on the way home, I get so angry with Leonore my whole body shakes. It's obvious that my relationship with Ben bothers her. What I can't figure out is why her reaction irritates me and gives me a kick at the same time. It occurs to me that maybe I actually like the fact that she might be seeing me in a new light.

~

Though we never officially talk about it, Ben moves into my place with his little plastic bag. I clear some space in one of my drawers and find an unused toothbrush and comb in my odds-and-ends drawer for him. Ben pretends he likes Optimus and Optimus starts peeing in Ben's brand new shoes.

18

To my delight, Ben cleans the flat every day and is careful with my things. Aside from a laminated photo of Arnold Schwarzenegger as Conan the Barbarian that appears on the fridge door one day, everything stays where it normally is and it even turns out that he's a fantastic cook. Ben tells me how as a six-year-old he'd already started watching cooking shows and trying to emulate the TV chefs by putting little salad garnishes on everything—which in Ben's case was grass that smelled of dog piss from the sidewalk outside their house in Burnaby.

On the way home from my work, we go to Billa and buy food. While I sit with a glass of wine in the kitchen, Ben chops vegetables or adds seasoning to some huge pot full of chili con carne or tomato sauce. Ben was horrified when he discovered that I cut everything with a blunt little knife, so together we bought a proper chef's knife.

"Now I don't look like a Yeti—and have started wearing shoes again—I was planning on trying to find a job," Ben says one day as he's standing there cooking. It's already pitch black outside. "I'll probably lose my mind if I just keep hanging around in your flat, and I've never been the type to live off someone else's money."

"I think Canadians are actually allowed to work in Austria," I say. "Legally I mean."

I've secretly looked it up on the Internet already.

Ben shakes his head. "Nah, real jobs are too hard to get," he says. "Some kind of under-the-table thing would suit me better. I've heard that if you stand outside the Polish church in the third district at 7 a.m. every Monday they come and pick you up. Then you get shipped out to some building site in the suburbs."

"Aha," I say and try to hide my disappointment. In my head it wasn't the sort of job I'd hoped he would go for. "Have you given any thought to that idea of going to school too?" I ask. "You could work at the same time as studying. Isn't there anything you're interested in?"

Ben doesn't say anything at first.

"Maybe something with cars," he says in the end. "I've always been interested in fast machines and stuff."

"There, you see?" I say. "Maybe there's some kind of foundation course in fast machines and stuff at the University of Vienna?"

"No, I'm not the school type."

"Give it some thought," I say.

Ben opens another beer. I try to stop myself from counting how many beers he must have drunk already today. *Nine.*

"What did you eat when you were homeless?" I ask.

"Always the best food," Ben says. "If you're going to steal, you might as well take the best stuff."

emmy abrahamson

"But you never got caught?"

Ben bursts out laughing, and nods as he carries on chopping celery. "Yeah, once, in Amsterdam. I made the mistake of stealing a frozen chicken and hiding it in my jacket. For two days I had to sit in a cell in a Dutch police station. But they were really cool. You were allowed to smoke ten cigarettes a day and you could use a little computer to watch TV or play Tetris. For lunch you always got white bread with sprinkles."

I listen to Ben's many stories, fascinated. Stories about the truck driver in Spain who invited him and The English back to his house and then wanted them to have sex with his fat wife while he watched. About the time a crazy Nigerian in Geneva took LSD and would have attacked a policeman with an axe if Ben hadn't stopped him. About the time he was woken up in the middle of the night by a toothless old drunk woman trying to have sex with him. About when he and The English found fifty euros on the street in Lyon and then went to a Chinese all-you-can-eat restaurant that threw them out because they ate all their food. A world that had existed in parallel to mine but that I'd been oblivious to. A world far away from my warm kitchen, which now has steamy windows and is full of the scent of fried onions, basil, and garlic.

When I notice that Ben reads next to nothing I take it upon myself to help him to discover the wonderful world of books. In secret, I buy books I think he's going to like and that aren't too hard. I start with some early Stephen King and Michael Crichton novels. I pretend to find them on the bookshelf and say, in a voice that's as nonchalant as I can manage, that he might find these ones interesting. When he starts reading and actually enjoys them, I feel like a proud librarian. The first book he ever reads on his own initiative from start to finish is Michael Crichton's *Jurassic Park*.

Because he hasn't seen many classic films either, we spend the autumn evenings watching *The Man Who Would Be King*, *Fitzcarraldo*, and *Don't Look Now*.

I take him to places in Vienna that he didn't know existed, like Hundertwasser's irregular, tree-studded building, the crypts under St. Stephen's Cathedral with their thousands of skulls, and the well-kept secret of Hitler's home in the sixth district. I show him where the resistance movement scratched messages during the Second World War, the "House Without Eyebrows" on Michaelerplatz and the place where W. H. Auden died just after a poetry reading. Because Ben won't take money from me, we go to second-hand shops and try to find him well-fitting clothes in good condition on the small budget he has. We hold a pretend funeral for his old clothes and burn them at a barbecue site on the Donauinsel. As the flames consume his jeans, T-shirt, and old boxers, we chant made-up Bible quotes while the Muslim family barbecuing a whole lamb next to us look on with curiosity. I manage what I never did with Matthias: I become Ben's Professor Higgins, and he my Eliza Doolittle.

19

I'd like to show you a bit of my world," Ben says suddenly one day.

"You don't have to do that," I say.

"No, I really want to," Ben says.

I try to stop the panic from showing in my face.

"No, honestly Ben, you don't have to show me your world. I'd rather listen to stories about it. I'm not adventurous by nature. There's a reason why I only use Facebook to stalk people and never write anything about myself."

"Facebook," Ben snorts. "Facebook's for idiots. Anyway, it would mean a lot to me if you wanted to meet some of my friends. We can go there now. Just go and see how they are."

"OK," I say, wishing we were already on our way home again.

We head out to the tenth district, where some of the streets look as if they haven't changed since the Second World War. The facades of the houses are covered in brown dirt and on the corner there's a bar—Zur Kneipe, written in black letters— where heavy dark-red drapes are drawn at all the windows.

The only things missing are a gang of small boys in shorts playing with a rusty bicycle wheel, and an air-raid siren.

"So is this the building you and the punks tried to squat in?" I ask.

Ben shakes his head.

"Nah, we got thrown out of there," he says. "It's a thousand times easier to squat in Amsterdam than here in Vienna. Strawberry's uncle owns this house and said we could live here until it gets torn down. So this is where I was sleeping after I lived in the bush—before I moved in with you."

"Strawberry?" I say. "There's a punk named *Strawberry*?"

To my surprise, Ben doesn't laugh.

"Why's he named Strawberry?" I ask a little nervously. "Did he do something awful—something to do with red stuff—so now he gets called it ironically?"

"I guess he likes strawberries," Ben replies. "That's not that strange, is it?"

We go into a building with an enormous metal door that squeaks as it opens. In the front hall there are a few empty buckets, and the stairs to the upper floors are cordoned off with hazard tape to show that entry is prohibited. Ben opens the door to the left on the ground floor and is immediately met with a noisy welcome. I take a deep breath and follow him. The apartment has dark wallpaper, a filthy floor, and the same smell Ben had on our first date, if a little less strong. It's as cold in the flat as it was out on the street, so there's probably no working furnace.

I'm introduced to three punks: Kobra, Vichor, and Strawberry. Although it's pretty much obligatory in Austria to shake hands with everything that moves, the punks just nod in my direction. I nod back. To my surprise, none of them have neon-green Mohawks or purple hair. Kobra's hair is dyed black, and Vichor and Strawberry have shaved heads. All three have black hoodies and jeans with horizontal tears— clearly the dress code of the anarchist world. Both Kobra and Vichor look older than I thought punks were allowed to be.

"What happened to your beard?" the one named Strawberry asks.

"I was sick of scaring young children," Ben replies.

"And are you living in the palace at Schönbrunn or Belvedere now?"

"Fuck off," Ben says with a laugh.

"Damn, it's great to see you again," Vichor says.

"You too," Ben replies.

Kobra, though quiet, is clearly the leader, closely followed by Vichor. Strawberry, nervous and jumpy, behaves like a dog that's so used to being beaten it goes mad with joy when its owner decides to stroke it instead.

Kobra slaps Ben enthusiastically on the arm. "Hey, we're gonna head out to the airport later," he says. "Fancy coming along?"

I can see how tempted Ben is to say yes, but he's already promised me we'll go food shopping on the way home. I've suddenly become the clichéd girlfriend, getting in the way of Ben's brief return to a wild single life. It makes my skin crawl. I'm torn between telling Ben to go with them, just to show how understanding and easy-going I am, and wanting to get him out of this place and away from these people as quickly as possible. But instead I just stand there a bit stiffly and try to laugh and look interested.

"Sorry," Ben says. "Maybe next time."

"What's he going to do at the airport?" I ask quietly when Kobra suddenly disappears into another room.

"That's how he makes a living," Ben says. "There's a couple of trash bins there that Kobra checks every other day."

"Why?"

"Loads of people throw their drugs away there before going into the airport and checking in. Stuff they'd be arrested for but forgot to leave at home. You can't imagine how many bags of pills, grass, and hash he's found there. Even cocaine sometimes. And mobile phones. I used to go along sometimes." Ben gestures through one of the doors.

"This used to be my bedroom."

I peer in through the door and see a drafty room where half the floorboards are missing. Apart from a chair and a pile of old newspapers, the room's empty.

"My soft mattress must be torture now," I say. "Was this where you slept on a tarp and cardboard floor?"

"That was in my bush in the Stadtpark." Ben's tone implies I should be able to keep track of his former sleeping spots. I've already noticed a shift in Ben's behavior towards me now that we're with the punks. It's as though he's mentally taken a step away from me and closer to them.

We sit on the sofa in the hallway, which seems to be the punks' gathering place of choice. There aren't any windows, and we're surrounded by no fewer than five doors. The sofa is the color of goulash and there are stains on it I decide I haven't seen. There's a bare light bulb hanging from the ceiling. I try to look as relaxed as possible, as though sitting on a soiled, stinking sofa is something I do every day. Everything around me is so dirty I'm almost on the verge of tears.

"Do you want some soup?" Strawberry asks.

"I'd love some," I reply.

He vanishes into the little kitchen.

"Strawberry always makes soups," Ben says, leaning closer to me and whispering: "He's always throwing up."

"Are the two things related?" I whisper back.

He shrugs.

"Why is he sick so often?" I whisper.

A moment later, Strawberry comes back with three cups of pale red soup. Although it's too thin and has an odd, metallic taste, I say it's nice. Vichor plonks himself down against the wall opposite us and Kobra sits cross-legged in the middle of the room and starts rolling a joint.

"Are you gonna go home at all?" Ben asks Vichor.

"You gotta be shitting me," Vichor says. "The fucking Austrians have stopped deporting me. I used to be able to just go and throw stones at a tram and the cocksuckers would send me back to Poland straight away so I could wash my clothes and get a decent meal at my mum's. But now they've stopped and my fucking ticket home's gone. No fucking way I've got the money to go home on my own. Dickheads."

Despite all the swearing, Vichor is smiling the whole time he's telling the story, and Ben is bent double with laughter beside me.

"And look at this," Vichor says, eagerly rolling up one of his pant legs.

"Stop showing that shit," Kobra mutters as he takes the first toke on his joint.

We lean forward to see what it is he wants to show us. Under Vichor's knee there's a wound that's at least fifteen centimeters long. There's a thick, festering scab and the skin around it is an angry red. Vichor looks at his shin with the same proud tenderness as a father looks at his newborn.

"Damn, what happened?" Ben asks.

Kobra picks a flake of tobacco off his tongue.

"I got in a fight with some dickhead," Vichor says with a shrug. "The wound wasn't healing and I've got no fucking health insurance, but around the corner there's a vet, and it says he takes 'animals big and small,' and fuck, I'm a big animal so I went in. The vet—he was actually pretty sound for an Austrian—said he could lose his license if he treated me. But his wife was a doctor—for humans—so he got her to prescribe me some antibiotics and clean up the cut."

Once again, Ben's been laughing throughout Vichor's story. I've been trying to laugh along. At last Vichor rolls his pant leg down again.

Half an hour later we're on our way back to the seventh because Kobra and Vichor are heading out to the airport and Strawberry's going to take a nap. My body feels oddly tense. Despite all the laughter, both on Ben's side and the punks', it was as though an invisible fog of aggression and bitterness pervaded the apartment. Also, the cold has made me stiff.

"Fuck, those guys are so cool," Ben says.

I nod.

He turns to me. "What is it?" he says. "I can see something's wrong. You've got that look on your face."

I don't want to bring the mood down, so I try to be as diplomatic as possible.

"They seemed really nice," I begin. "It's just that it was like I didn't exist."

"What do you mean?"

"Ben, didn't you notice that they didn't ask me a single question or even seem to notice I was there? I was like the invisible non-punk. It might . . . some people . . . would interpret that as a bit impolite."

Ben looks genuinely surprised.

"Strawberry gave you some soup," he says at last.

"It would have been rude to give you soup without giving some to me," I say. "But I realize they're probably suspicious of people who aren't punks. And who have jobs and clean clothes. I guess I'll just have to wait for next time to ask Vichor what he actually thought about the Kokoschka exhibition."

"There's no goddamn way Vichor would go to a Kokoschka exhibition," he says, irritated.

"I *know*," I say and try to stop myself getting angry too. "I was trying to lighten the mood." I smile at Ben but make my voice serious. "So, Vichor, would you agree that Kokoschka demonstrates that a flight from reality does not lead to freedom?" I pretend to reply as Vichor: "Fuck, that dickhead Wittgenstein was right when he said Kokoschka lays bare people's emotional skeleton. Like Strawberry. If Kokoschka'd painted Strawberry, he would have transliterated his spiritual life as a hunched figure on a puke-green background. But hey, what the fuck, I've gotta go and throw stones at some old ladies now."

"Stop it."

"Sorry," I say. "But they really did ignore me."

We sit on the tram, which begins to travel through the dark tunnels by Matzleinsdorfer Platz.

"You didn't ask them any questions," he says suddenly.

"Of course I did," I lie. "Ben, admit it: they're weird and impolite."

"You don't know anything about these people. Kobra was in prison for *five years*. He was accused of throwing a TV at a police officer. But it wasn't him."

"That's what all the TV throwers say."

"It wasn't him," Ben repeats. "And the police officer was paralyzed from the neck down. But Kobra wasn't a snitch. They're great guys. You just think anyone who didn't go to university is an idiot."

"I don't think that at all," I say. "But I think people are happier if they can choose what career they want to have and you can do that with an education. You have more options. The world's hardly crawling with earthworm pickers who love their jobs so much they never want to retire. Which they wouldn't be able to do anyway since they won't have any pension after working under the table all their lives."

We pull into Kliebergasse Station, where the walls are covered with posters for Verdi's operas, ballet performances, and an exhibition of the Russian Tsar's family jewels at the Albertina. Streaks of dirt coat the posters, which have so many layers under them that the corners have started to crinkle up.

"Do you think *I'm* an idiot?" Ben asks me.

"Of course I don't," I reply. "But people who throw stones at trams are."

"Just so you know, I've spent my whole life working. It's only the last year that I've been traveling around. And when I work I'm always good at what I do."

"I haven't accused you of anything. Relax."

Ben grunts something in response and stays in a bad mood for the rest of the day. I don't know if his irritation is directed at me or at the punks, but it's the last time he suggests we go and see them.

20

One Wednesday morning, I'm sitting with one of my favorite students. Edeltraud is around seventy and has decided to spruce up her English. Four years ago her husband died—at the same time she was diagnosed with colon cancer. Since her recovery, she has taught street kids in Kathmandu, learned to play the harp, gotten a tattoo of a blue morpho butterfly on her shoulder, and soon she's going to start Finnish classes.

"Which household remedies help with colds?" I ask as I try to conceal a small yawn. We're currently going through chapter seven of the *Berlitz English Level Four* book, "Illness and Household Remedies." Outside a police siren wails.

"Personally I prefer a large glass of Glenmorangie," Edeltraud sighs. "Do we have to continue on with this chapter?"

There are only ten minutes left of the lesson, and until I meet Ben, so I'm happy to skip the jaunty lines about garlic, chicken soup, and steam baths that chapter seven boasts. Edeltraud takes a magazine out of her bag.

"In the *New Scientist* there's an article about the liquid

methane gas on one of Saturn's moons," she says. "I didn't understand all the words, but perhaps you could help me?"

Outside, I hear yet another police siren, followed by a third a couple of seconds later.

"Of course," I say.

There's a light knocking at the door.

"Yes?" I say.

The administrator, Dagmar, sticks her head in. In the staff-room there's a rumor going around that Dagmar gets turned on by stationery and Mike says he once saw her stroking a red Bic pen in a way that just felt wrong.

"I just wanted to say everything's OK," she says. "Stay where you are and carry on with the lesson."

"What's happened?" I ask.

"A robbery," Dagmar replies.

"Oh no, they haven't taken the grammar books, have they?" I exclaim.

Dagmar looks at me blankly. There's also a staffroom rumor that Dagmar has undergone a long, complicated procedure at the general hospital to remove her entire sense of humor.

"Not here," she says. "On the other side of the street. There's nothing to worry about. Just carry on with your lesson. But stay back from the windows. And unfortunately we have to remain in the building until it's all over."

"OK," I say.

As soon as Dagmar has closed the door, Edeltraud and I rush over to the window. From our fourth floor vantage point, we can see five police cars parked on an otherwise empty Mariahilferstrasse. Twenty men dressed in black with the word COBRA in white across their backs have surrounded the Erste Bank across the street. The bank I once went into to fill out a withdrawal slip to calm myself down.

"I wonder how many robbers there are?" I say.

Both Edeltraud and I crane our necks to see more, in vain. The black-clad Cobra officers spread into a semi-circle formation. Further down Mariahilferstrasse, I can see the police trying to hold back curious onlookers. Many of them are holding up their phones to film the drama.

"Amateurs," Edeltraud says.

"Why do you say that?" I ask.

"Everyone knows the best time to rob a bank is on a Monday morning," Edeltraud replies. "No one expects to be robbed then. Austrians always get it wrong."

"I don't agree with you. I love Austrians," I say as we sit watching the drama outside. "OK, they can be a bit arrogant and unfriendly sometimes, but they really know how to enjoy life. A good glass of wine, finishing work early on a Friday, opera, theaters, delicious baked goods, all the Christmas markets, Müller Rice with cinnamon, Eurovision singers with beards, the beautiful countryside, the fact that there are vineyards within the Vienna city limits, the ice cream parlor on Tuchlauben. And there's a sexy kind of decadence here, as though we're all going to live forever or die tomorrow. I wouldn't want to live anywhere but Vienna."

"Austrians close their eyes to the world around them," Edeltraud says bitterly.

Both Edeltraud and I jump when the bell rings to tell us the lesson is over, and I remember I'm supposed to be meeting

Ben. Which is impossible at the moment, because we're not allowed to leave the building.

"Have you ever been robbed?" I ask Edeltraud.

"Only in Brazil," she says and holds up her fingers. "Three times. One time at a restaurant, once while I was swimming with a couple of other tourists in a lagoon, and a third time when the police stopped the taxi I was in."

"The police?"

Edeltraud nods.

"The police robbed me," she says. "And you? Have you been robbed?"

"Yeah, by one of the ice cream parlors by Schwedenplatz," I say. "I paid for three scoops of ice cream but I only got two. They never gave me my strawberry scoop. Bandits."

Suddenly there's the sound of gunshots from the bank. The Cobra officers immediately crouch down and half of them press themselves against the outer walls of the bank. One of them waves at the building we're in to say we should get away from the windows. An ambulance and two more police cars arrive. From the other classrooms I can hear that everyone else is ignoring Dagmar's and the Cobra officer's orders as well.

"Julia!" I hear suddenly.

Edeltraud looks at me, but I don't know if I heard right.

"Julia!" we hear again.

"In here!" I reply.

The door is thrown open and Ben marches in. In three long strides he is by my side and embraces me with a long kiss.

"You're OK!" he exclaims, relieved.

"Of course I'm OK," I say.

Ben shakes his head. His forehead is shining with sweat.

"I had no idea what had happened," he says. "I was on my way down Mariahilferstrasse when a man in black with a submachine gun started shouting at me in German that I couldn't go any further. Since all the police cars were outside the language school, I thought something had happened here."

"Like what?" I say. "A student going berserk?"

"Who knows? Maybe he got annoyed about some verb or comma or whatever it is you do here. I'm so glad you're OK. If you'd been hurt I would've ripped their scalps off."

"There's a robbery across the street." I gesture at the bank.

Ben looks out of the window. "Cool," he says. "I hope the bank robbers win."

I suddenly remember Edeltraud, who's staring at Ben.

"Edeltraud, this is Ben," I say.

"Hi," Ben says, and they shake hands.

Edeltraud nods at the street.

"But how did you get into the building?" she asks.

"I got into the backyard and then climbed up a drainpipe," Ben says. "For a while I thought the pipe wasn't going to hold but luckily it was all right. A nice woman on the second floor let me in when I knocked on the window. And then I ran up here."

"My hero," I say.

Dagmar sticks her head into the room again. At first she looks a bit surprised to see a strange man standing beside me and Edeltraud, but she quickly adjusts her expression to something she probably thinks of as "efficient yet accommodating."

"We're closing the school," she says. "They're saying this could go on for hours, so for everyone's safety we're closing for the day. We'll have to leave through the back."

She disappears again.

"Doesn't it feel like being sent home from school when it snows?" Edeltraud says merrily.

"I was one of those kids who loved school," I say.

"Did she say through the back?" Ben asked.

"Yes, through the back onto the street behind us," I say. "Although I prefer your dramatic route up the drainpipes and through someone's private apartment, Spiderman."

Ben looks a bit crestfallen but then claps his hands together.

"In that case I have to at least carry you out in my arms," he says.

I shake my head. "I'd rather walk. But thanks."

"You can carry me out," Edeltraud says.

Ben scoops her up immediately, and she yelps in delight.

"Spiderman, Spiderman, does whatever a spider can . . ." Ben sings as he runs out of the room with Edeltraud in his arms.

I gather my books and stuff them into my bag, smiling.

~

During our next lesson, Edeltraud asks where one might find someone like Ben.

"In a bush," I reply, and think it's probably time for my friends to meet Ben after all. And for him to meet them.

21

Leonore's holding a premiere for *Closer*. She's both directing it and playing one of the lead roles. It will be the first time Leonore and her theater crowd have met Ben, and I've also persuaded Rebecca to come with Jesus-Jakob. Ben's freshly shaven and showered, and I've made sure he's wearing his best clothes.

"Can't you wear the other jacket?" I say when it's time to put our coats on.

"I like this jacket," Ben says.

"It looks a bit uncool. Take the other one we found in the charity shop."

"I like this one," he says with a tone that indicates the discussion is over.

As we walk towards the little theater, the first snowflakes of winter start to fall. Ben doesn't seem too enthusiastic about going to the theater and instead is looking longingly at the small wooden huts on Graben, where they're selling Christmas punch and glühwein.

"Do we have to watch the whole performance?" he asks.

"Once we've thrown our rotten tomatoes at the actors we'll probably have to run out as soon as possible," I answer.

"Really?" Ben says.

"Idiot," I say and smile at him. "Who knows, maybe you'll love the play. It's full of sex and smut and drama."

He doesn't look convinced.

Unfortunately, *Closer* isn't good. At one point, a set panel falls off the wall for no reason, the lighting is confusing, and the four actors seem to think they're in four different plays. Ben starts laughing out loud in the scene where Leonore does a pole dance that's meant to be seductive, and everyone turns around to look at him. The elephant in the room is that Leonore has given herself the role of the young girl rather than the role Julia Roberts played in the film version.

When the play is finally over, everyone piles into the little foyer bar where complimentary Red Bull is being served. There are metal trays of dried-out canapés and cocktail tomatoes filled with some kind of salmon-pink cream. The Beige Man stands in a corner not talking to anyone.

"Rebecca, this is Ben," I say. "Ben, Rebecca."

"Nice to meet you," Rebecca says.

"Likewise," he says. "Please tell me you hated that as much as I did. Julia's too kind to admit how terrible the play actually was."

"It was pretty horrible, wasn't it?" Rebecca says in a half-whisper and leans closer to Ben.

I can see she approves of him. But on the other hand she'd probably approve of anyone who wasn't Matthias, whom she always openly disliked.

When Leonore comes out of her dressing room I give her the bouquet I brought with me and tell her how wonderful she was. Since Ben moved in with me I've stopped going out with Leonore and the mood between us has become frosty to say the least, as though my new relationship is a personal betrayal.

"It went well, didn't it?" Leonore says, with a self-confidence you can't help but admire.

"Leonore, this is Ben. Ben, Leonore."

Ben and Leonore shake hands. It's hate at first sight.

"So you're the homeless guy who's moved in with Julia?" Leonore says.

"Yep," Ben says. "And you're the terrible actress with the rich husband?"

"Leonore, you were absolutely fantastic in the play!" I say, alarmed.

Then, luckily, someone else comes along to congratulate Leonore and I take Ben by the arm and lead him over to a corner.

"You shouldn't have said that!" I hiss. "She's a friend. Are you crazy?"

"She's not your friend," he says. "And why would you even want to be friends with someone like that?"

"B-because . . ." I start to stammer. "You can't only have best friends. Like you and The English. Sometimes you need friends you don't like quite as much."

"No, you don't."

"Yes, you do," I say. "Otherwise you end up with only one friend. And then that friend leaves or dies and then you don't have *any*. You need half-friends!"

Ben looks at me angrily.

"Stop being so Swedish."

"*So Swedish?* What do you know about Swedes? I'm the only Swedish person you know."

"You shouldn't be so fucking weak," Ben clarifies. "Grow some balls."

"Well firstly, I hate language like that," I whisper angrily. "And secondly, I really hate language like that."

"People like that are just using you. You're a thousand times better than someone like Eleanor."

"Leonore," I correct him.

"*Whatever.*"

"Just because you've slept on a tarp it doesn't mean you can ignore social norms. That you have the right to be some kind of Buddha of truth. Because you don't."

"You're a coward."

"A coward?"

I notice the couple next to us glancing over so I lower my voice.

"A coward?" I repeat.

"OK, maybe not a coward," Ben says. "That was the wrong word. But you live your life so fucking safely. I've seen how you never take any risks."

"And that's news? I told you that the very first time we were on the Donauinsel that I don't like surprises. And what's so bad about never taking any risks? I crossed the street on a red light the other week and you know what happened? I was shouted at by some old Austrian guy. Even though the street was empty. There were no cars!" By now I'm hot all over. "I'm actually so sick of the myth that adventurous people are somehow better than the rest of us. That you're only worthy of attention if you've swum naked in the Ganges or stroked a dolphin. 'Oh, look at me! I'm covered in mud at a music festival where there are no toilets. I'm so cool!'"

We're both quiet for a moment. I can see the Beige Man talking on his phone with a serious expression. If Ben and I hadn't been arguing I would have made a joke about a Red Bull crisis—"we've run out of wings"—but now I don't say anything.

"If there's anything else about me that bothers you, you may as well say it now," I say in the end.

He looks at me.

"You seem to be allergic to having the windows open. The flat's always so stuffy."

"Allergic to open windows?"

Ben nods.

"You'd probably be happiest living in a barrel," he says.

"Fresh air is overrated," I mutter.

"And sometimes you go to bed really early. A grown woman shouldn't be going to bed at 9 p.m."

"A grown woman can decide for herself when she goes to bed," I hiss. "All the cool people go to bed early. Because we know the value of a good night's sleep. And you can read before you fall asleep. Only losers stay up all night."

"*Whatever,*" Ben says again. "Leonore's a desperate cow anyway."

"And you were a smelly tramp when we met," I say. "So there."

It's our first fight. For several minutes we stand next to one another and drink our Red Bull without saying anything.

"Shall we go?" he says eventually.

I look at him.

"I really don't want to fight with you," he says.

"I don't want to fight with you either," I reply.

"That performance has made the evening bad enough."

"Come on."

On the way home, Ben has me in stitches by imitating Leonore's pole dancing around a lamp post. Around us, the streets are completely covered with snow.

22

A survey," I say eagerly, and point.

Ben and I are at the Christmas market at Spittelberg, each holding a dark-blue mug of steaming glühwein. The Christmas market at Spittelberg is one of my favorites. No tourists find their way there, as it's hidden on a few streets in the middle of the seventh district. So instead of tourists, the market is full of students, young families, and Viennese hipsters—the kind that sit in front of a laptop in an empty office with wooden floors where there's nothing but an enormous inflatable Heineken bottle or some other postmodern irony. It's well below freezing, and steam comes out of people's mouths. There's such a crush that we have to stand really close to one another, something I have nothing against.

Ben is freshly shaven, which always makes his eyes look even bigger, and I can't get enough of looking at his face. I notice several women ogling him, which makes me feel quite pleased with myself. Then I wonder whether there might be a business opportunity in creating an online dating site for women in their thirties and homeless men. *What David lacks in teeth, he more than makes up for with his ability to drink antifreeze.*

Ben looks at a group of high school students with sagging backpacks who've just invaded the market.

"Teenagers," Ben observes, and shudders. "Maybe they can tell us why they're selling wooden statues from Bali, Peruvian wool hats, and incense at a Christmas market?"

"For someone who was sleeping in a bush not so long ago, you can be surprisingly conservative sometimes," I say. "Do you want another?"

I hold up my almost empty cup. Actually, the glühwein tastes sour and cheap, but I'm determined that we're going to have a nice time. After the Christmas market, the plan is to go to Kent, a Turkish restaurant in the sixteenth. Ben is friends with one of the waiters there, who's invited him to his cousin's wedding and offered him smuggled cigarettes from Ankara.

"Sure," Ben says. "My treat."

He gets a few coins out of his pocket and starts counting.

"No," I say quickly. "I'll get them. It's OK. Same again?"

"No, let me pay," he says, tetchily.

"No, it's OK. Stop it."

"You paid for the last round," he snarls. "I should have enough."

"Honestly, Ben, it's no problem. Stop it."

"No."

"Stop it!"

"Let me pay!"

"HI!"

Suddenly two teenagers are standing next to us, and Ben

and I both jump. There's a girl and a guy. The guy has acne on his cheeks and the girl has long blow-dried hair.

"We're from the international school here in Vienna. Could we ask you a few questions?" the girl says in English and goes on without waiting for a reply. "Question number one: are you from here?"

"No," Ben says.

"Yes," I say simultaneously.

The girl looks at us, a little confused. The guy taps out our answers on the iPad he's holding. The girl looks quickly at the nest question.

"Are you on holiday in Vienna?" she asks.

"No," I say.

"Yes," Ben says.

The girl reads the next question: "To reduce the amount of litter on the streets, would you be willing to work as green volunteers and collect litter?"

"No way," Ben says.

Both teenagers stare at him. The girl's cheeks get a little redder.

"But there *is* no litter on Vienna's streets," I say. "It's one of the world's cleanest cities."

"It's a *hypothetical* question," the girl says, like she's speaking to a five-year-old. I already know she's the kind who always emphasizes the word "maybe" and loves bringing up Julian Assange.

The girl reads the next question from the iPad.

"What do you think is the best way to reduce the amount of garbage?" she asks.

"Provide more trash bi—" I begin.

"Beat up anyone who litters," Ben says.

The guy with the acne grunts in agreement and notes down Ben's reply.

"Can you think of anything that would make the world a better place," the girl asks, "from an environmental perspective?"

Ben nods enthusiastically. "Stop saving the pandas. The only reason pandas are still alive is that people think they're cute. They cost millions of dollars to protect, and are weak by nature. Pandas are meant to die out. Put money into something else. Write it down. Just the way I said it."

The guy is typing as fast as he can. The girl is staring at Ben. Her teenage world has clearly been reconfigured.

"Thanks for your time," the girl says and pulls the guy away, although he's still in the middle of writing.

When the teenagers have gone I turn to Ben.

"You forgot to say how much you hate seal pups and starving African children," I say.

"And that I support cancer," he says.

"But don't say people should be beaten up."

"Why not?"

"It makes you sound like a Neanderthal. There are better ways to communicate with people."

"Not with idiots," says Ben.

Inwardly I sigh, but I choose not to continue the discussion.

"Wait here," I say, and go and buy another two mugs of glühwein.

To my relief, Ben doesn't protest this time.

After another glühwein and a Christmas punch I've

stopped feeling the cold, and the people around us have lost their outlines. It's no longer as packed at the market; many people have gone home for dinner.

"One more of these," I say, holding up my mug, "and you might get to see my impression of Falco singing 'Rock Me Amadeus,' which not enough people have heard. Wait, are you wearing the red T-shirt?"

Under Ben's jacket, I've spotted something red.

Ben nods.

"But it was dirty," I say. "I've been sleeping in it the last few nights."

"If a girl wears an item of clothing it's automatically clean for at least another week," Ben says. "Didn't you know that?"

"No, but it sounds logical," I say in a voice that's perhaps a little too loud. "Look, there's one of my students over there."

I point at Vera, who's standing with a little girl and looking at a purple scented candle in one of the stalls.

"Go and say hi," Ben says.

I shake my head.

"Students always seem to be confused when they see me outside the classroom," I say. "As though I shouldn't exist when I'm not teaching. But let me take the mugs back so we can get our deposit. Then we should probably go to Kent. Everything's gotten a little . . . a little . . ."

I leave the sentence unfinished because a sour taste has suddenly invaded my mouth. Instead I take Ben's blue mug and steer myself with unsteady steps towards the glühwein stall.

"Hi, Julia!"

Someone taps me on the shoulder. It's Vera.

"Vera!" I say. And then again: "Vera!"

"This is my daughter, Sabine," Vera says. "Sabine, this is my English teacher, Julia."

I shake hands with Vera's daughter, whose hair is in two thin braids. I hope neither Vera nor her daughter notice that I have to concentrate hard on standing upright, and that my breath stinks of cheap red wine.

"Are you buying birthday presents?" I ask.

The taste in my mouth is getting worse. Suddenly an unappetizing smell of currywurst hits me.

"We're looking at potential *Christmas* presents, yes," Vera corrects.

"And did a Nicholas visit your school last week?" I continue in German to Vera's daughter, whose name I've already forgotten. It's a tradition in Germany and Austria for St. Nicholas to visit children on the sixth of December.

Vera's daughter looks at me with a stony face. "*St.* Nicholas visited us," she says. "Not *a* Nicholas."

Now I see the man beside us bite into a currywurst, making diarrhea-yellow mustard ooze out the other side of the sausage and bun.

"Yes, of course," I say, before vomiting elegantly into one of my dark-blue mugs.

I stand still. Vera and her daughter stand completely still. Everything happened so fast and so smoothly that if I wasn't holding a mug of vomit in my hand, I wouldn't have believed it had happened.

"Excuse me," I mumble and turn around.

As quickly as possible I go back to Ben, put the mugs on the street, and pull him away from the Christmas market while I try to fight back the tears.

"Ben, I just vomited in front of a student," I cry, miserably.

Ben roars with laughter. "Did you?"

I nod. "In a glühwein mug," I sob.

"Well aimed," Ben says. "But now we probably can't ask for our deposit back. That's ten euros gone up in smoke."

Now we're on Burggasse. The pedestrianized street has been sanded, but I still seem to be struggling to get a footing and have to cling to Ben.

"You don't get it," I say. "I *vomited* in front of a student."

Ben shrugs.

"Shit happens," he says. "How are you now?"

"No, it can't happen!" I say. "Students think we're robots. We're not allowed to be human. And definitely not human in a disgusting way. I had a math teacher once who farted in front of the class and he was forced to move to another school because no one could ever take him seriously again. A school *in another country*."

"Stop caring so much about what people think of you. Who gives a shit?"

"I give a shit. *I* do. This is your fault!"

I cling to Ben again as we go up the street. Paranoid, I keep looking around in case Vera, or some other student, comes rushing towards me.

"Why is it my fault?" Ben says.

It's so cold that I notice for the first time how red his ears have become.

"Because I don't usually drink that much glühwein," I say. "I've started drinking so much since we got together. How can you not be drunk?"

"It takes a bit more than four small cups of mulled wine

to get me drunk," Ben says gloomily. "Don't forget I used to polish off a bottle of cheap red before breakfast when I was sleeping on the streets."

My stomach makes a gurgling sound and once again my mouth fills with the taste of sour wine mixed with cloves.

"I'm not feeling well," I say. "I think we might need to go home."

"Sure," Ben says, disappointed.

I almost step in dog shit.

"All these stinking dogs in the seventh!" I say. "God, I'm going to puke again. And we haven't even eaten dinner yet. Even though we usually always eat dinner. That you've cooked. Oh God, are you a feeder?"

"What's a feeder?"

"Someone who gets turned on from seeing other people eat," I say, getting more and more het up. "People who get a sexual kick when their girlfriends start weighing five hundred kilos and get rolls of fat on their rolls of fat. You're a feeder! And you've started cooking all the dinners."

"I cook all the dinners because the only thing you can cook is pasta with pesto," Ben says. "And that weird goat's-cheese salad. Apart from that, you seem to think all food can only be cooked on the highest heat."

"The highest heat is the only heat," I slur. "The others are just there for appearances' sake."

Ben unlocks the outer door and the temperature goes up by several degrees as soon as we're inside. Oddly, the warm air makes me feel even more ill, and everything has started spinning. When we get to the second floor I point to the door on the left.

"ELFRIEDE JELINEK," I whisper.

"Don't yell," Ben says.

I clap my hands over my mouth straight away. Then I open them and make them into a little funnel.

"Elfriede Jelinek," I now whisper through the funnel.

"I don't know who that is," Ben says.

"Je-li-nek. The Nobel Prize winner. *The Piano Teacher*. *Bambiland*. *Women as Lovers*."

Ben shrugs his shoulders, which for some reason makes me very, very angry. In some part of my brain I add Austrian glühwein to the list of alcohol that makes me very, very angry and should therefore be avoided in the future. The list already features whiskey and wine from south Sweden.

"You are *so* ignorant," I say angrily. "There's a Nobel Prize winner living in our house. A NOBEL PRIZE WINNER. A WINNER OF THE NOBEL PRIZE. THE SWEDISH NO-BEL PRIZE. FROM SWEDEN. JELINEK. You ignoramus."

Doggedly we carry on up the stairs, though the whole world has started swaying a little too much for my liking and my head aches. The acrid taste fills my mouth.

"There's probably a lot *you* don't know," says Ben. "Like what a Buick Grand National is."

"I know enough to know I don't want to know what a Buick Grand National is," I say, now on all fours, since it seems the safest way to get up the stairs.

"So who's ignorant now?" Ben says. "Come on, I'll give you a hand."

I wave his hand away.

"No, I can manage," I spit and crawl further up the stairs. "Up to my barrel."

~

When I wake up the next morning, Ben has put a glass of water and two aspirin on the bedside table. On the floor by the bed there's a bucket, which is mercifully empty. The whole flat has been cleaned, the laundry has been hung up on the rack, Optimus has been fed, and the toilet smells of air freshener. To my surprise, Ben has also put all the shoes in the hall in size order. When I thank him, he says he can't take credit for the shoes, since it was actually me who arranged them once I'd finally managed to haul myself up the stairs and into the flat.

23

Ben and I are pretending to be Mikhail Baryshnikov and Anna Pavlova on ice. Now that the Christmas market has closed, there's an enormous skating rink in front of the town hall. Great plastic snowflakes hang in the trees and the town hall is lit up purple. Although it's almost nine-thirty in the evening, the rink is still full of people. Classical music plays from the speakers, which suits our made-up jumps, steps, and pirouettes perfectly.

"I think I have to rest a bit," I say when we stop in a dramatic pose. "Then we should play Nancy Kerrigan and Tonya Harding."

Ben grins before pushing off with his left arm forward and his right leg backwards. I try to skate to the ramp at the side without colliding with too many people. This evening is a bit different, because Ben has paid the entrance fee and for the skate rental. He's got a job via the Poles in the third district. Before that was a failed attempt as a ticket seller for Mozart concerts—a job that most of the desperate, half-decent-looking guys in Vienna can get. All the Mozart costumes were too small for Ben and he kept telling the tourists to go to the other Mozart concerts because they were better. After two weeks he'd only made twenty euros because it was on commission. But now he's got a job as a plasterer.

"They're a real bunch of bloodsuckers," Ben says. "An Austrian would have got twenty euros an hour for the work. I'll get eighty cents a square meter. So even if I have to plaster a 100-square-meter house three times over, I'll only get eighty euros. But it's a job."

"I'm so proud of you," I say.

"Don't say that."

"Why not?"

"If I was five and had made you a nice picture out of pasta shapes, you could say you were proud," Ben says. "This is a crappy job. But it will be great to finally be able to pay for food and so on."

As I stand on the ramp, trying to wiggle life into my frozen toes, I spot Karen, who also works at Berlitz. Karen is so thin and pale that several times students have asked whether she was ill. One student even started bringing in sandwiches and oranges for her.

"Hi, Karen!"

Karen catches sight of me and comes over with a large bag in her hand.

"Have you finished or are you about to start?" I ask.

"I'm going home now," she says. "Are you on your own?"

I shake my head and point at Ben, who's stopped being a ballet dancer. Instead, he's doing a robot dance in the middle of the ice with two children who are cracking up with laughter. For a long time, Karen and I just stand staring at him.

"Hey, I actually wanted to ask you something," Karen says after a while. "Would you be interested in teaching an evening course at the university? It's a beginner's course I generally take care of, but I'm busy at the moment."

"The University of Vienna?" I ask. "Absolutely!"

"Great," Karen says. "The course doesn't start until September, but they pay three times more than Berlitz."

"Wow, thanks!"

"And soon I'm going to have loads of university essays to grade if you want a few," she says. "It's well-paid too but I won't manage them all."

When Karen leaves I can't stop smiling. A university job. At Berlitz I've also started getting a higher hourly rate because I've taught more than three thousand hours. And to put a cherry on top, I had a great idea today for a story about a Catholic priest and a girl in Australia. And I even know what the priest's name is going to be: Father Ralph. Which is odd, actually, because I've always thought Ralph was a bit of a dorky name, but an author must listen to her instincts. What a beautiful, heart-breaking novel it's going to be! I make my way over to Ben on the ice rink.

"Ben! I'm going to start teaching English at the university!" I shout.

"Come here, university professor!"

Ben lifts my right hand and I do a pirouette. When he lets me go again, I say: "I'm probably not allowed to call myself a professor just because I'm teaching an evening course, but it's still cool."

"The plasterer and the professor," Ben says.

"I don't know if professors are allowed to go out with plasterers," I tease him.

"Sorry baby," Ben says, lifting my hand so I can do another pirouette. "You're stuck with me for the rest of your life."

~

It's not the wild times with Ben that I like the most; it's the quiet, daily routines. Eating breakfast together, going to Billa or Merkur Market to do the shopping, or sitting on the sofa in the evening—me with a glass of red wine, and him with a glass of beer (now that I've convinced him that there's no law that says you have to drink straight from the can), and eating Lindt chocolate with salted caramel. It's in those moments that I feel such joy and satisfaction, a peace like never before. Part of me starts hoping that Ben might really have forgotten about Berlin.

"Bubbles should ditch that loser Johnny," Ben says. "He'd be much better off without him."

"Johnny's going to be Bubbles' downfall," I say. "Without giving too much away."

Since Ben's never seen *The Wire*, we've started working our way slowly through all five seasons, and suddenly we're talking about McNulty, Kima, Omar, and Herc as though they were personal acquaintances.

"Pawel at work was telling me you can go skiing just an hour from Vienna," Ben says suddenly.

"I know," I say. "At Semmering."

"Why've you never mentioned it?"

"Because I'm not interested in skiing," I reply.

"But we have to go there!" Ben exclaims. "If it's so close to Vienna. Pawel said I can borrow his cousin's snowboarding equipment and everything."

I don't answer at first.

"Hmm . . . I don't know," I say in the end. "The sight of me plowing down the slope at five kilometers an hour might be a bit too much of a turn-on for you. I don't know if you'd be able to handle it."

"It will be really fun," Ben says enthusiastically.

"OK," I reply. "We can go there on Saturday. But only as long as you promise not to paint white streaks under your eyes or leave me on my own at the top of a slope."

"Deal," he says.

Then we watch yet another episode of *The Wire*.

Later, as we brush our teeth, we have a discussion about whether D'Angelo Barksdale should have snitched on Avon or not.

"You just don't snitch," Ben insists. "Never ever."

"Is that a rule in the underground?" I ask, lowering my voice dramatically. "Never snitch! Are there any more rules you follow?"

"Me? I'm not in the mafia."

I rinse away my toothpaste.

"No rules then," I say. "But things you do and don't do? In the homeless world?"

Ben ponders.

"I guess they'd be always sharing your alcohol when you have it, never taking anyone else's sleeping spot, and never, ever speak to the police."

"It sounds like the Berlitz world," I say eagerly. "We always share the blue Murphy's *English Grammar in Use* book because it's the best; we never take someone else's student, and we never, ever talk to Dagmar. The similarities are frightening."

We turn off the lights and go into the bedroom.

"What does 'effervescent' mean?" Ben asks as we lie in bed reading.

"To be lively or enthusiastic," I reply. "Aren't you the native English speaker?"

"Yeah, I guess I am," Ben says with a sigh.

"If you'd tried a bit harder in school, I think that maybe you might have known something like that," I say, half-joking.

"Yes, Mom," Ben says, sighing again.

I try not to be bothered by his comment.

"And speaking of mothers and things mothers have to put up with but not people like me," I say, "would it be possible for you to stop leaving your dirty T-shirts all over the apartment?"

Ben sighs again before replying.

"Yes," he mutters, then fixes his gaze back on his book so I'll understand he doesn't want me to disturb him again. And I almost get the feeling he was about to add "Mom" again, but caught himself at the last minute.

24

The next Thursday is exhausting because all my students are new and at different levels. One woman—Level Three—can't stop talking about the place she and her boyfriend have just bought. I already know there's Italian marble in the bathroom, no fewer than two balconies, and a lift that opens straight into the flat.

"And it's one hundred and twenty . . . how do you say *Quadratmeter*?" she asks.

"Square meters," I reply dully.

The woman beams.

"Yes, one hundred and twenty square meters," she says. "And in the first district."

"How nice," I say, wishing she would stop going on about her flat.

"My boyfriend is the vice-CEO of Hewlett-Packard here in Austria," she says, positively glowing.

For a few seconds I wonder what it would be like if I had a boyfriend who was vice-CEO of Hewlett-Packard. And how it would be to not have to pay for nearly all the food, not to mention owning a flat together.

"He must spend a lot of time at work," I say, trying to find something negative.

The woman shakes her head.

"Not that much," she says. "And we always make sure we take really, really nice holidays. Last winter we were in the Maldives."

"Oh," is all I can think to say.

Because I've heard enough about the woman's fantastic apartment, boyfriend, and holidays by this point, I force her to do an incredibly boring exercise on adverbs.

For the last three lessons, I have a particularly unpleasant man with strawberry-blond hair. Despite the fact that he's an AMS student, for some reason he's been put into private lessons rather than being taught in a group with other students. We've just read an article in *Passport*.

"What's a 'behemoth'?" he asks, pointing at a word in the magazine.

For a moment I wonder whether I can bluff my way through an answer, but I'm too tired to come up with anything. Ben snored last night. Something I've noticed he does when he's drunk a whole lot—and since he's been working as a plasterer for the Poles, he's been drinking more than usual.

"I actually don't know," I say. "But I'll look it up during the break."

The man looks at me with disgust.

"You don't know?" he says.

Now I know why the red-haired man doesn't have lessons

with other people. So he won't be hit over the head with a Level Six textbook.

"If I were to guess from the context of the word, I'd say it was something highly negative," I say to try and save the situation. "The word definitely doesn't originate from English."

"As my English teacher, how can you *not* know what a word means?" the man repeats.

I suddenly feel a desire to get home to my apartment as soon as possible. Away from idiots like this man. Away from Berlitz and away from the whole world. An empty apartment where I can be alone and not have to talk to anyone.

"Everyone's human," I say, trying to smile. Then I say the sentence I often find myself saying to students: "Teachers aren't dictionaries."

"Is it true that you come from Sweden?" the man says. "And not from England? That English isn't even your native language?"

"If you turn to page thirty-seven, we can . . ." I say, trying to hide the fact my voice is shaking with anger.

But the man refuses to give up.

"If you don't know what the word means," he says, "then I think I'd like to request another teacher."

I want to shout that he's not even the one paying for these lessons, the Austrian state is, so how dare he be so demanding?

"Just because I don't know what a 'behemoth' is?" I ask.

"Is Ken free at this time on a Thursday?" the man asks. "I've heard he's supposed to be good."

"I'll check with the secretary," I say.

When our lesson is finally over I sit for a while. Luckily, no one needs the room. I stare ahead of me and wish intensely I was able to be home alone in my apartment. Just for a few hours. Or maybe even a few days. Right now I don't feel like talking to anyone or listening to anyone else talk, not even Ben. After twenty minutes I get up and fetch my jacket from the staffroom.

When I get home I take a little breath before unlocking the door.

"Hello?" I call, hoping Ben's still at work.

"I'm here," Ben replies. "In the living room."

I take my shoes off and notice that one of Ben's black socks is on the hall floor. The one with the big hole that shows his heel—which he so proudly calls "his onion" when he shows off his foot. I pick it up and go into the living room.

"I found this by the shoes," I say.

"Oh, sorry," Ben says. "Throw it in the laundry basket."

He's sitting at the table with my laptop, and on the screen I can see some kind of racing game on pause.

"I found this totally cool driving game completely free on the Internet," he says. "You get to drive round the Nürburg-ring track."

My annoyance immediately increases by a factor of ten.

"I never said you could install anything on my computer," I say.

"Why are you in such a bad mood?" Ben asks.

"I'm not in a bad mood," I say, trying to control my voice. "I'm just a bit tired and I would appreciate it if you could ask me first before installing something on my laptop."

I go into the bedroom to put his sock in the laundry basket and wish I could just sit alone on the sofa with Optimus and watch TV. Instead it feels like I'm being suffocated by Ben's presence. On the bedside table I see an empty Ottakringer can. I pick it up and storm back into the room.

"Do you have to leave beer cans all over the apartment?" I ask angrily, putting it down in front of the laptop.

"It's just one can," he says. "God, you really are in a pissy mood!"

"Didn't I just tell you I'm not?" I say. "It's just kind of gross, coming home to an apartment strewn with socks and beer cans."

"Gross?" Ben repeats. "Don't make out like your shit don't stink."

His words make me explode.

"You are *so* horrible sometimes," I hiss. "I'm not the one who's eaten dog biscuits for no reason, or who wipes their fingers on their socks while we're eating. *Wipes their fingers on their socks.* Do you realize how disgusting that is? Sometimes I look at you and I'm just ashamed!"

Ben doesn't say anything, but his face has become a shade darker and his eyes harder.

"And sometimes I even get the feeling you get a kick out of showing how gross and proletarian you are," I go on. "And I *hate* it. Not to mention how you behave towards my friends. You act aggressively and provocatively, as though you want to give them a reason not to like you before they really find a reason not to like you."

"All your friends are idiots," Ben says, through gritted teeth. "Apart from Rebecca."

"Oh yeah, and The English is such a goddamn philosophy professor."

"The English did actually study philosophy," Ben says. "For four years."

"Everyone who studies philosophy is an idiot: it's just a waste of time with no future. It's like studying *The Simpsons*. And I don't want to talk about The English, I want to talk about the fact that your behavior is totally unacceptable. I deserve better than this. Than *you!*"

Ben turns his gaze back to the laptop.

"I thought we were 'equals' who walked 'side by side,'" he says in a put-on voice.

"Are you kidding?" I ask. "My equal? Do you seriously think you are *my* equal? Is that the joke of the century? And you know something else? I don't like that tongue thing you do in my butt. I JUST PRETEND TO LIKE IT."

I rush into the bedroom and slam the door shut. Forty-five minutes later I come back out because I've calmed down. I also need to piss, which for a split second I was considering doing in the plant pot with the peace lily in it so that I wouldn't have to leave the bedroom, before I realized I was actually ready to apologize.

Ben is standing in the kitchen, making chili. I don't know whether his cheeks are red from the steam or something else.

"Sorry," I say.

"Me too," he says, but his voice sounds weird and cold.

"I love you," I say.

"I love you too," he says with the same weird voice.

It's the first time we've said it and the mood couldn't be less loving.

"And that stuff about the tongue thing," I say carefully.

"I'm not always pretending. Sometimes I like it. Or . . . I don't mind you doing it. When you do it."

"It's OK," Ben says, focusing hard on opening a can of black beans. "I won't do it again."

"That wasn't what I meant."

"It's OK," Ben repeats, moving on to a can of red kidney beans.

I stand at the door and watch him stir the contents of the cans into the big pan.

"Oh God, I had such a terrible student today," I say and start telling Ben about the red-haired man.

I know I'm going to have to do my dancing monkey act for the rest of the evening to make up for my outburst, and I'm willing to. While we eat, the mood—slowly and with lots of strained jokes from my side—becomes more normal, and after dinner we watch two episodes of *The Wire* and eat Lindt chocolate as per usual.

~

The next day at work is much better. I only have three groups and one of them is Bettina, Steffi, and Hans.

"The homework was a bit hard you give," Steffi says to me.

"The homework I *gave*?" I correct her gently. "Why did you think . . ."

Suddenly I freeze. Just as I knew several months ago that Ben would be waiting for me outside the school instead of at Starbucks, another realization hits me now with the same force and clarity.

When the last lesson is over, I rush up Mariahilferstrasse, down Stiftgasse, through Burggasse and finally up Neustiftgasse. My throat is burning from the running and my back is damp with sweat. As soon as I get into my house I rush up the stairs so fast I stumble and hurt my knee. The Serbian super mopping the stairs asks if I've injured myself. I shake my head and say it's just a graze, though my knee is throbbing and tears well up into my eyes.

I dash into the apartment and run to the bedroom.

"Ben!" I call.

But I already know.

He's gone.

25

What are you doing?" Rebecca asks nervously.

She has found me crouching by a bush, my cheeks tear-stained. She is holding two dark-blue tote bags full of English textbooks, which means that she must have come straight from Berlitz after reading my text message.

"I'm trying to find Ben," I say as I wipe my face and get up to check the next bush, even though it's already pretty obvious it doesn't contain a six-foot-five man.

It's grown dark and the snow has turned into small, hard bullets of ice. Aside from the streetlights, Stadtpark is completely dark and unwelcoming. Now and then a plaintive quacking can be heard from the deep, stinking lake in the middle of the park. Of all the parks in Vienna, Stadtpark has always been the one I've liked least, because of all the duck shit and random bums. The irony of fate has now brought me here to search for my own bum.

"But I can't find him," I say in a trembling voice.

A used condom glimmers between the leaves and the bush

stinks of piss and human excrement, which makes me recoil. I turn to Rebecca.

"I can't find him," I repeat and start crying again.

Rebecca gently leads me to the nearest bench, and we sit down.

"Maybe he's been in an accident and been taken to the hospital?" she suggests.

"I've called the general hospital and checked the whole hospital system and they can't find him," I sob.

"Or he could have been arrested?"

"But then he would have called, right?"

"Not if what he's done is so awful he doesn't want you to know about it."

"Like what?"

Rebecca doesn't answer, but gives me a look that could suggest anything from stealing a Kinder Egg to necrophilia.

"And you've called him, of course?" she asks.

"He doesn't have a phone," I say. "And I don't know what his email address is, if he even has one."

"Facebook then?"

"He's not on Facebook. He says Facebook's for idiots."

"But you're on Facebook."

"And?"

"Didn't it annoy you a bit that he called everyone who uses Facebook an idiot if you're on Facebook?"

"To be honest I don't care enough about Facebook to be hurt," I reply.

I don't want to have a conversation about Facebook right now. I just want to talk about Ben because if I talk about him he's not gone.

"I just don't understand," I say.

"If he's left you because of that argument he doesn't deserve to be with you," Rebecca tells me.

"No," I say, shaking my head. "It's me who doesn't deserve him. He was always so kind and happy and crazy about me and I was just embarrassed and angry with him all the time because of—what? Because he had no education? Because he didn't have a job that was cool or prestigious? I've destroyed the best thing that's ever happened to me because of a sock and a beer can. Because I'm a stupid fucking snob."

"Don't say that," Rebecca scolds.

"And now he's gone and it's my fault. I'm such an idiot."

We sit there in the dark as I sob and snot all over Rebecca's coat.

"You're not an idiot for wanting something better," she says, her arms still around me.

"I'm such an idiot," I repeat.

The sleet continues to fall and the only sound is the muted traffic on the distant road.

~

The next morning I go to the tenth district where Kobra, Vichor, and Strawberry live to see if Ben is there. But where the building once stood, there's now a chasm of gravel and bricks surrounded by a rickety fence.

26

The days come and go and I find new reasons to explain why Ben's gone. He decided to hitchhike to Berlin after all. He met an old friend. He got some last minute job outside of Vienna from the Poles. He's planning a really, *really* exciting surprise for me! But none of the reasons ring true.

The days become weeks. I start to wait. And wait. And turn into a robot. I go to work, I teach, I go to the gym, I wait for the tram, I feed Optimus, I clean my ears with a cotton swab. I do all the things I usually do. At the same time, every atom in me is screaming: WHERE IS BEN? On the shelf in the bedroom are his T-shirts, which I carefully folded after washing them. In the kitchen drawer, the knife we bought together lies on a checked dishtowel. In the sink there are some dark bristles I can't bring myself to clean away. On a shelf in the living room, there's a couple of crumpled old receipts and three coins. On the bedside table, Stephen King's *Night Shift* lies open. Everything is as it should be. Apart from the fact that Ben's not there. The only one who's happy is Optimus. Like a forgiving former lover he starts nudging his nose under my hand again, and scratching his litter with extra enthusiasm every time he's in the tray.

I start to miss Ben so much it becomes hard to concentrate on anything else. I remember all the reasons I actually love him: because he accepts me completely; because he thinks the Erasure song "Always" is the most beautiful song in the world but would never admit it to any of his guy friends; because I never have to pretend to him; because he seems to think everything I do is fantastic; because he thinks, just like I do, that halloumi is overrated and that capoeira is silly; because he's tall and sexy; because he's not a bit ashamed of the fact he worships Arnold Schwarzenegger; because he reminds me of the cool guy in school who always found people like me insipid; because we had a whole conversation a few weeks ago in pretend Portuguese; because he's the only person I've ever met who dreams every night that he's a superhero; because the sex we have is amazing but it never lasts long once I start thinking about whether it's time to clean the fridge; because he makes me laugh; because I make him laugh; because he loves *Labyrinth* as much as I do; and because all of life's colors have become much brighter since I met him.

And then comes the letter.

I don't even see it at first because for some reason it's tucked into an ad from Billa announcing an offer on *Ja! Natürlich* fruit yogurt for €0.59 and Emmentaler for €1.29. It's not until I put the leaflet in the kitchen so I can use it under Optimus's litter tray that I notice it. It's addressed to Ben and it's the only letter he's ever gotten since he moved in with me. I see the dark-blue logo on the envelope and my heart starts to beat faster. I rip open the envelope and read that Ben has been accepted into the foundation course in mechanical engineering at Vienna's *Technische Universität*. He'd sent in the application a few weeks before our fight.

27

I go out with Leonore again. It's ball season and there are young girls and women in long dresses and rock-hard hairdos everywhere, shivering in the cold. For the next two months, the staple diet of Vienna's population will be prosecco and *Krapfen*, the sweet doughnut with apricot jam inside.

Leonore and I are in a bar in the Metropolitan Hotel, which is clearly the place to be right now. According to Leonore, anyway. Just like Optimus, she looks at me with a forgiving, yet condescending gaze.

"I was thinking of putting on *The Vagina Monologues*," she says. "All the proceeds will go to the women's shelter in the thirteenth."

"Isn't *The Vagina Monologues* a bit passé?" I ask. "A bit nineties maybe?"

Leonore looks at me.

"How could it ever be passé to fight for women's independence and liberation?" she says.

Something hot and red explodes inside me.

"Fight for women's independence and liberation?" I repeat. "You're not going to go out and fight the Taliban in Afghanistan, you're going to stand on a stage for two hours and talk about vaginas. In a show that centers on quite brutal sexual experiences and which is incredibly negative about sexual relations between men and women. And which has that tasteless monologue about 'a good rape' a thirteen-year-old is exposed to. I hate *The Vagina Monologues*!"

Leonore looks at me without blinking. I've even managed to surprise myself. Truth be told I don't even have anything against *The Vagina Monologues*.

"Are you some kind of anti-feminist?" she snarls.

"Oh no, Leonore, my secret's out," I say. "You're right: I hate all women. Damn me if we don't all belong in the kitchen."

The last thing I want is to go back to my flat, so why am I trying to sabotage the evening?

"Maybe we should go home now," Leonore says, her voice laced with frost. "I have to get up early tomorrow."

"No! Please, stay," I say. "Sorry I was a bit short. Of course you should put on whatever you want. You would make a fantastic . . ." I try to say the word as normally as possible ". . . vagina."

Leonore brightens up immediately.

Five minutes later she takes my arm.

"Hey, what happened with that guy . . . what was his name again . . . who was living on the street?"

"Simon," I say, because Leonore knows perfectly well what his name is.

"No? Was it really Simon?" she says. "What happened to him?"

"He had to go to Amsterdam for a while," I say.

"Aha," Leonore says and then starts telling me about the trip to Hawaii that she, the Beige Man, and their son have been planning for the Easter holidays.

When we're at Passage an hour later it feels like I'm in some awful déjà vu which not even the huge quantity I've drunk can shake off. Everything is the same, and yet not. Because Ben came into my life and now he's gone. The floor inside Passage is covered in brown pools from the ice that's melted off everyone's shoes, and the air is more humid than normal. I buy Leonore and myself a cocktail. Around me, several of the men are in tails and their hair is slicked back, which means they must have escaped from some nearby ball. Someone taps me lightly on the shoulder. It's Mike, the actor from the language school.

"Hi, Julia."

"MIKE!"

I throw myself on him and kiss him twice on the cheeks. Even though we saw each other at work a couple of hours earlier and have never kissed each other on the cheek before. This evening seems to be full of surprises.

"Do you come here often?" Mike asks and looks around.

"Is that your best pick-up line?" I say in a deep voice and try and give him a seductive look.

"I-I . . . it-it wasn't a . . ." Mike starts to stammer.

I give him a punch in the arm.

"Relax," I say. "But honestly: what *do* you say when you're trying to pick someone up? Ask what the time is, or what?"

Mike thinks a while.

"I probably just ask what her name is," he says. "Have you

heard that our branch of Berlitz might be closing and moving somewhere else? Apparently the rent's too high."

"No, Mike! No!" I say angrily. "No work talk. Naughty boy! Now I want to get to know the person-behind-the-actor-behind-the-English-teacher Mike. Or the actor-behind-the-person Mike. The person-behind-the-person Mike. Mike person: who are you?"

Mike stares at me. But the last—and biggest—surprise of the evening still awaits. I have sex with Mike.

28

You scratched me," Mike says.

Mike is sitting beside me on the bed, trying to feel his back. I don't say anything because I'm hoping that if I just keep my eyes closed he'll disappear. That if I really, really concentrate, I can make him dissolve into thin air.

"I think it might even be bleeding," Mike goes on.

I screw up my eyes even harder. *Focus, woman, focus!*

"Oh God, you didn't give me a love bite did you?" Mike says.

I glance at Mike and see how he's feeling his neck with his fingers as though I'd left a love bite in braille.

The sex was mediocre at best. Both Mike and I were pretending we were more attracted to one another than we actually were. When Mike took his T-shirt off I noticed he had long dark hairs growing randomly on his chest, and three birthmarks in a row under one of his nipples, like Orion's belt. In the end I was forced to close my eyes and imagine it was Ben in front of me.

"You were pretty wild," says the-person-who's-still-next-to-me. "I never would have thought it of you."

Instead of leaving, Mike does something much worse. He crawls up behind me and puts his arms round me like a clingy little monkey. I open my eyes and stare ahead of me. I have to strain every muscle to stop myself from pushing him away. Ideally through the window.

"I thought maybe after we'd been to sleep we could eat breakfast at Wirr and then take a stroll in Schönbrunn," Mike muses contentedly. "And Burg Kino might have a matinee playing. I have to warn you in advance that I always have to have popcorn when I go to the movies."

I almost fly up out of the bed.

"Mike, sorry, but you have to go now," I say, trying to put on as many clothes as possible as fast as possible. I would gladly have put on my jacket, shoes, scarf, hat, and gloves before rushing out of the door, but unfortunately we're at my place.

"But it's three in the morning," Mike says.

"Vienna's one of the safest cities in the world," I say. "Steer clear of men standing beside open vans offering you sweets, and nothing will happen to you, I promise."

"I don't even know if there are any buses running now. And it's cold outside. It's started raining."

"Mike, you're not made of sugar, and you have to go. I have a boyfriend. No, a *fiancé*. We're going to get married."

At first, Mike doesn't say anything. Then he checks under the covers. Then under the pillows. Then behind the curtains before he picks up the little grey stuffed rabbit that sits on the bedside table and holds it up.

"Hi, I'm Julia's fiancé," he says in a high, girly voice. "She hugs me really hard while we eat chocolate and watch *Sex and the City*."

To begin with I don't know how to react. I'm too tired, drunk, and grossed out. The only firm thought I can muster is that *Sex and the City* hasn't been on for over ten years, so his insult is nothing other than ridiculously inaccurate.

"What?" I say. "Put the rabbit down."

"If you have a fiancé, where is he?" he asks. "Your relationship status on Facebook says 'single,' so how can you have a fiancé?"

Ben was right. Facebook is full of idiots.

"And why did you sleep with me?" Mike continues.

I don't respond.

"What a horrible fiancée you are."

"Give me the rabbit," I say.

Mike throws the rabbit at me. Just then, Optimus struts into the bedroom. With a soundless leap he jumps up onto the bed and starts nosing Mike.

"Where did you come from then, little pussy-wuss?" Mike says. "What a cute little pussycat you are. Pusskins."

Optimus settles in Mike's arms and starts purring.

"Optimus, come here!" I say. "Optimus."

Judas starts to purr even louder.

"Optimus, heel! HEEL!"

Mike and Optimus carry on cuddling. In the end I walk over and grab Optimus out of Mike's arms. With a loud meow he tears himself from my grasp and runs out of the room.

"What kind of person are you?" Mike says, staring at me. "First you're unfaithful to your fiancé and seduce me, then you torture your cat."

I pick up the rabbit and throw it at Mike.

"Get out of my flat!" I bellow.

Mike puts his clothes on. With a certain satisfaction I see that I actually have scratched his back so hard it's bleeding.

"I have to borrow your toilet," Mike mumbles at the front door.

"OUT!" I shriek and push him through the door.

It takes me a long time to fall asleep. When I finally drift off I sleep so deeply that I don't hear my mobile when it rings.

29

I stare at the number.

00160468530238

Twice someone has tried to call me. All mobile numbers in Austria start with 06 and ordinary numbers start 01. This one's too long, and it has two zeros at the beginning. Suddenly my stomach ties itself into a little knot. I run over to my computer and write the numbers in. 001 604 is the international code for Vancouver in Canada. Someone in the room starts shrieking uncontrollably with joy.

For the next three days I refuse to leave the apartment. I tell Berlitz I have the flu, and to Rebecca I claim exceptional circumstances and tell her she has to buy some Whiskas chunks in jelly for Optimus and milk, bread, and Portuguese red wine for me.

"You know it's a *mobile* phone?" Rebecca says gently. "That you can take it out with you?"

She sits beside me on the sofa. The mobile lies before us on the coffee table.

"You don't understand," I say.

I've hardly been able to tear my eyes from the phone the last few days and I carry it from room to room. Even when I'm on the toilet. If I were to have a shower there'd be a risk I wouldn't hear it ring, so my hair is dirty and my pajamas have begun to emit a ripe aroma. Over the last three days I've also discovered a whole new world of daytime TV. A world consisting of trashy German soaps with names like *Tempest of Love*, and folk-music shows in which the male presenters wear lederhosen and hike across green meadows in the mountains. I also discover that the Norwegian Eurovision star Wenche Myhre is still alive, and appears to have a blossoming career in the German-speaking countries.

"Have you tried calling back?" Rebecca asks.

"More or less every ten minutes, but no one picks up," I say. "And now I just get a busy signal all the time."

"But what if it's not him?"

"I don't know anyone else from Canada," I say. "I know it's him. I just know it."

"What if Ben gave your number to someone he knows in Canada," Rebecca suggests. "And now that person is trying to get in touch with him."

I fall silent.

"I hadn't thought of that," I say. Then I shake my head. "No, I know it was Ben trying to get hold of me. I just *know* it."

Then she says the unsayable:

"But if Ben is, or was, homeless, how did he have the money to go back to Canada? And why hasn't he tried to call again?"

I don't answer. We sit there in silence, still staring at the mobile phone.

After another two days, I'm forced to leave the apartment. Rebecca says she refuses to support my self-imposed Kasper Hauser–existence and the toilet paper's run out. My fledgling friend Elfriede Jelinek would never have been such a traitor.

With a frown etched onto my face, I run down to Billa, buy food and toilet paper, and rush home again, even though I've taken my mobile with me. When I'm on my way up the stairs it rings. It's Rebecca.

"Hi," I say.

"Don't sound so disappointed," she says. "I've found the address."

"Which address?"

"The address for the telephone number. The address Ben called from."

"What? Rebecca, thank you thank you thank you!!! But how did you manage it? I could only see that the number came from Vancouver, no more."

"I had to do a bit of searching," Rebecca says. "I couldn't find out who lives there, but Ben definitely called from 1348 Commercial Drive, Vancouver."

1348 Commercial Drive. 1348 Commercial Drive. 1348 Commercial Drive, I repeat to myself.

"You can even look at the address on Google Street View," Rebecca goes on. "It looks quite nice."

Rebecca's right. When I look up 1348 Commercial Drive I can see a wide street with green trees and several shops. On the right side there's a place with a black canopy called Caffé Amici. 1348 Commercial Drive. A wave of joy and calm sweeps over me now I've finally found a lead that might take me to Ben. It's as though my lungs have filled with air again.

"Rebecca, I need a favor," I say. "Can you look after Optimus while I go over there?"

She is smart enough not to try to change my mind. Instead, she asks direct, practical questions.

"Wouldn't it be better and cheaper to wait and see if he gets in touch again?"

"I can't wait any longer," I say. "This waiting is driving me mad."

"But what if he was calling to break up with you?"

"Then at least I'll know," I say. "I'm going to Canada. I've actually always wanted to go there. Up to now I've never had a reason, and I haven't had a proper holiday in ages, and I have the money to do it. And if I find Ben I can apologize for the horrible things I said and tell him I know he'd decided to go back to school."

I can hear how tackily desperate I sound, and the sensible side of me whispers: *don't go*. But I choose not to listen. Having something concrete to do after waiting around for so long feels wonderfully liberating.

"But isn't it all a bit Glenn Close in *Fatal Attraction* to go halfway around the world on a hunch?" Rebecca asks.

I don't reply. *Don't go.*

"Imagine if you go and he's there with his wife and three kids. A wife whose name is Shania or Melody or something like that."

"Well, for one thing, I know he won't be," I say. "And for another, at least then I'll have some answers. After I've killed

Shania. Anything's better than not knowing." I'm silent for a few seconds. "Something must have happened. I have to at least try to find out what it is."

~

Six days later I'm sitting on a British Airways flight on my way to Vancouver.

30

The plane is full to bursting. Even though I had a window seat on the flight to London, after my connection I've somehow ended up by the aisle with two people between me and the window. The seat feels hard and cramped and however much I twist and turn, I can't get comfortable. There's also so little legroom that my knees are forced up against the seat in front of me and I'm struggling to find space for me, the blanket, the earphones, the socks, the earplugs, the menu, and the little pillow British Airways has given me since I boarded the plane. I end up sitting with a whole pile of odds and ends on my lap, making it impossible to put down the tray table in front of me. A couple in their fifties are seated next to me, not saying a word to each other. The woman is reading a paperback and the man is staring straight ahead of him. The other passengers have already got their headphones on and are watching the screens in front of them.

I sink down into my seat and wish Ben were with me. Since Ben left I've had almost daily conversations with him in my head. To cheer myself up I think about the silly things

Ben used to say: like his opinions about Tina Turner ("Is it just me, or has she always been sixty years old?"); hippies ("I've never met a hippy who wasn't a tight-ass."); Penelope Cruz ("She reminds me of a cockroach!"); and soups ("Soup is the future."). They're ridiculous little things that make me laugh and which I would never tell anyone else, precisely because they're so ridiculous and trivial. I am already looking forward to the day I can stamp on a cockroach and tell Ben I've killed a "Penelope Cruz." I smile to myself, but not even my memories of Ben can make the time pass more quickly. Instead I start watching a romantic comedy starring Kate Hudson, but unfortunately the film makes me want to stick sharp objects in my eyes. From all over the enormous plane I can hear groaning, coughing, throat-clearing, sighing, quiet conversations, and the odd snore. It's not until the first meal is served that everyone comes back to life again.

"Here you are," the baritone voice says, setting down a dark-blue tray of food in front of me.

There's a surprising amount of food on the tray, and it even looks quite appetizing. Suddenly, the man next to me turns towards me.

"Can you see what they've done?" he says.

I notice how his wife rolls her eyes before focusing all her attention on the food.

I look down at my tray. "It looks quite good," I say.

"But can you see what food they've given us?" the man says.

Once again I look at my food and try to solve the mystery. The man points with his white plastic fork.

"White bread, pasta, red meat, and a dessert packed with

sugar," he says. "Food that is guaranteed to give us constipation." He leans closer. "Airlines do everything they can to stop us going to the toilet. Especially when it comes to number twos. *Everything.* With this kind of food they'll make us as constipated as possible. I bet you've never thought of that."

The man gives me a satisfied little wink and then starts spreading butter on his little roll.

Constipation or not, I eat up all my food, more to pass the time than from hunger.

After the meal, coffee is served. When the man beside me has had his plastic cup filled with coffee, he turns towards me again.

"Causes constipation," he says, pointing at the cup.

I smile and make a little hurrah sign.

"What takes you to Canada?" he asks then.

"A friend. And you," I nod at the man and his wife, "are you from Canada?"

"Oh yeah," the man says. "From Kelowna. It's about three hours drive from Vancouver."

"Have you been on holiday in England?" I ask.

"No," the man says, and suddenly our conversation is over.

I get out the Lonely Planet book on British Columbia that I bought at Heathrow. It's the first time I've been to North America, but after being force-fed a diet of American TV it almost feels like I've had a parallel life there. At least in the States. I don't know as much about Canada, but I have seen *Ice Road Truckers*. And when I was little I devoured all the *Anne of Green Gables* books, which was the start of my desire to one day visit Canada and drink "raspberry cordial soda," whatever that is, just like Anne. For almost two hours

I read about what you should do in the event of a bear attack, and about places called Kamloops and Banff, and I admire the photos of snow-topped mountains.

Suddenly it's time for the next meal. Because the man next to me and his wife have fallen asleep, I'm the only one eating. After passing through so many time zones, I no longer have any idea whether the meal is breakfast, lunch, or dinner.

I try to sleep but fail. On the little TV screen that shows the flight route and the exact position of the plane, I can see that right now we're over the open sea. It makes me think of the beginning of a gripping story that I absolutely must write: about a group of schoolboys whose plane crash-lands on a desert island. But before I get any further I realize with a sigh that William Golding has already written *Lord of the Flies*. Ben's right, perhaps I should try and write something that's closer to my own life.

I go to the toilet to stretch my legs. Outside the toilets, several people are standing around looking like miserable Ghosts of Flights Past. The steward is whispering to one of his colleagues as they prepare some flasks of coffee. Somewhere on board a baby starts to cry. The air in the plane feels more and more stifling with every minute that passes. The cabin crew come round with water and orange juice.

Over the next few hours, I can barely sit still, and my legs hurt so much it's almost unbearable. We're served yet another meal. My claustrophobia grows. I try to sleep, but can't manage it this time either. My seat has turned into a prison in miniature. The Lonely Planet book gets boring. I stare at one comedy after another without actually watching anything. My legs are throbbing with pain now. This journey is never going to end. And then suddenly, the plane starts its descent.

31

The man gives me a nudge with his elbow and nods towards the window.

"British Columbia," he says, as though the plane's destination had hitherto been uncertain.

I strain my neck to see out through the window. All I can see are brown forests.

"I thought there were mostly pine trees in Canada," I say.

"They are pines," the woman says.

It's the first thing she's said throughout the whole journey.

"But they're brown?" I say.

The man and the woman look at me and nod.

"*Oh yeah*," the woman says. "That's the pine beetle, it's killed all the trees. It's probably killed more than half the trees in British Columbia. Some people say it's the world's worst insect plague. And the winters these days are never cold enough to kill the beetles off."

I'm almost too shocked to speak. Outside on the ground there's still nothing but brown forests, as far as the eye can see.

"So all these forests are dead?" I ask.

The man and the woman nod again.

"But why isn't anyone writing about this?" I burst out. "This is world news! The world's biggest insect plague. Half of the forests are dead. It's *terrible*."

The woman shrugs.

"Oh, no one ever writes about Canada," she says.

I give the Lonely Planet book in my hand and its photos of dark green forests an angry look. For the rest of our descent I refuse to look out of the window in shock and in protest against the pine beetle and British Columbia's dead forests.

At last we land and, like a herd of zombies, everyone staggers off the plane. My legs are hurting so much I would have crawled out along the boarding bridge if I could. Outside it's overcast, and a clock inside the airport says it's twenty to eleven. I stand still for a while, trying to figure out whether it's twenty to eleven in the morning or the evening. After the long journey and over twenty-four hours with no sleep, time has become a slippery, confusing concept. On tottering legs I start to move in the same direction as all the others. A wave of mild nausea washes over me.

"Passport, please."

I give my passport to the stubbly man behind the bulletproof glass and try to smile at the first Canadian I meet in Canada. He doesn't smile back.

"What's the reason for your trip to Canada?" the man says.

"I'm visiting a friend."

"What is your friend called and what's the address of his or her place of residence?"

"It . . . he . . . is called Ben Richards and he lives at 1348 Commercial Drive. Here in Vancouver."

Am I imagining things or did the man react slightly when I said Commercial Drive?

"What kind of friends are you?"

I almost want to turn around to the traveler behind me to ask whether the man is really allowed to ask me that. But instead I lean closer to the bulletproof glass so that only he can hear me.

"We're lovers," I say and blush, more from anger over the personal question than from embarrassment.

The man looks at me for a while.

"Where have you flown from?"

"Vienna," I say. "In Austria. I had a stopover in London."

"Why did you fly from Vienna if your passport is Swedish?"

"I live in Vienna."

"What is your occupation?"

"I'm an English teacher."

"Do you intend to work while you are in Canada?"

"No," I say. "Canadians already speak such good English."

I already realize it was a mistake to try and joke. The man with the stubble looks at me.

"Are you being insolent?" he asks.

I quickly shake my head and my cheeks grow hot.

"Sorry," I say. "Not at all. I'm not intending to work while I'm in Canada. Sorry."

"How much money do you have on you?"

"I-I have two hundred Canadian dollars with me in cash," I stammer. "And my Visa card."

"How did you obtain the money?"

"Human trafficking in Moldova," I say. Not. Instead I say: "Working as an English teacher. At Berlitz. I am, as I said, an English teacher."

When I've finally got the stamp in my passport and am allowed to go and fetch my bag, my legs are shaking. I'm dismayed at the way the Canadian people have treated me so far. In my head I get mad at Ben for the fact that Canadians are not as friendly as he's always claimed, and in my head Ben assures me that I just happened to meet a twat who gets a kick out of being an asshole towards other people.

My nausea gets worse. After collecting my bag I come out into an enormous hall and try to find the train that goes directly to Vancouver. My relief at being in Canada is wrestling with the exhaustion and the jet lag that seems to be getting worse with every minute, and everything feels a bit surreal. I'm sure I'm talking too slowly when I ask the woman at the information desk where I can buy a train ticket. Suddenly I'm struck by a terrifying thought. *I'm upside down. Vancouver is on the other side of the globe. I'm upside down. Or inside out. Or the other way around. Or something. Everything. Is. In. The. Wrong. Place.* I'm on the verge of falling to the ground and hanging on for dear life, and it's only with the greatest of effort that I manage to sit down on one of the blue seats on the train. Even though I've never taken LSD, I realize this must be what it feels like. *How can everyone around me be pretending that this is normal?* Stiffly, I hold onto the armrest of my seat to stop myself flying up to the ceiling. Or down to the ground.

32

Itry my hardest to admire the city, the skyscrapers, and, in the distance, the snow-topped mountains, but I fail; instead I spend the whole train journey fighting my nausea and my hallucination-like jet lag.

I make my way to the Buchanan Hotel, where I've booked a room for seventy-nine Canadian dollars a night. There's a bed with a chintz quilt, a table, a closet, a TV, and a tiny little hand sink. Matching chintz curtains hang at the windows. The shower and toilet are shared with two other rooms on the same floor. It's surprisingly quiet around me.

I mustn't sleep. All the travel guides recommend adjusting to the local time immediately. Since it's not yet two o' clock in the afternoon I have to make sure I have no chance of being horizontal, and I don't want to go to 1348 Commercial Drive before I've had a good night's sleep, so I decide to go and explore Vancouver.

"Would you like a map of the city?" the man at reception asks as I go by.

I shake my head.

"Thanks, I have this," I say, holding up the Lonely Planet book.

I wander for hours around the city. In Stanley Park I admire an enormous totem pole, and in the West End, the skyscrapers. Everything seems strangely familiar. At first I think it must be my jet lag playing tricks on me, before I realize I actually have seen all these places before, because every single American B-movie ever made was obviously shot in Vancouver. Despite my preconception that all North Americans are overweight, the people I see are normal, even suspiciously sporty.

The sky stays gray, and for half an hour it drizzles. I buy a cupcake and a little thimbleful of wheatgrass in an effort to blend in with the Vancouverites. My feet are aching but I keep walking, because I know I'll immediately fall asleep if I go back to the hotel. I walk all the way to picturesque Gastown and look in a few galleries showing masks made by the indigenous population.

Then I turn a corner and everything changes.

The street before me is full of zombies. Skeletal figures shuffling along aimlessly. Everyone is gray and most of them are staring at the ground. Some have shopping carts full of bulging plastic bags. A sickly-looking man comes towards me in his motorized wheelchair, and if I hadn't jumped aside he would have driven over my feet. Stupidly, I carry on down the street rather than turning around. Half a dozen people in rags are gathered on every corner. Some sit on boxes, talking to each other and exchanging cigarettes. A man in a long dirty coat asks me something I don't understand. I pass another man with a tattoo on his forehead who's injecting a needle into the neck of a woman lying on the ground. The woman's eyes are closed.

"Oh my God, is she all right?" I cry.

The man ignores me.

"Are you OK?"

I almost jump when someone touches my arm. It's a sturdy woman with a face like a moon. On her light-blue wind-cheater it says "Vancouver Volunteer Corps."

"I'm lost," I say.

"Where's your hotel?" the woman asks.

"In the West End," I say.

The woman takes me by the arm and starts leading me in the opposite direction.

"Come on, we'll find a taxi for you," she says briskly. "Do you have enough money for a taxi?"

I nod.

"What is this place?" I ask.

"Downtown East Side," the woman replies. "Also known as Junk Town, Skid Row, Crack Town."

"So many junkies," I exclaim.

"They're harmless," the woman says as we head down the street. "At least in the daytime. It's the drug dealers you need to watch out for."

"But why don't the police do anything?"

A man with a bare chest is pushing a stuffed shopping cart. He greets the woman.

"Hey, Al," she says to him. "What can they do? There are too many of them. That's why we help."

I think about the tattooed man and the woman lying on the ground.

"Junkies aren't the smartest people in the world," she continues to me. "If they were they wouldn't have become junkies in the first place."

The woman sticks her arm out and a taxi pulls up alongside us. Dusk has started to fall.

"West End," the woman says to the taxi driver when he winds down the window.

"Thanks so much for your help," I say.

"Have a lovely stay in Vancouver," the woman replies with a smile.

Then she turns around and goes back the way we came. She looks relieved to have gotten rid of me.

The taxi driver asks where I'm from.

"Vienna," I reply.

"Oh, those canals," he says and sighs longingly.

33

The young couple is standing outside the McDonald's on Commercial Drive. They're holding one another's hands and watching the people eating inside. The girl has short hair and a long, rainbow-dyed dress; the guy has a ponytail and flared jeans.

Suddenly they start banging on the windows of McDonald's.

"Pigs!"

"Nature-wreckers!"

"Murderers!"

"Hypocrites!" they yell.

Several of the diners inside McDonald's look up to see where the noise is coming from.

"Do you know what you're eating?" the girl shouts.

"How can you eat at this horrible place?" the guy shouts. "Don't you know McDonald's is destroying the rainforest?"

"Of all the places on the Drive you came here?"

"You're eating our planet!"

I'm touched by the couple's passion. I grew up as part of

a generation that takes passivity for granted, and my eyes fill with tears at their energy and their entreaties. It's almost as though I align myself with them, even though my protest would be of another kind.

"Stop using 'I'm lovin' it' as a slogan!" I would be screaming. "You never use the progressive present tense for emotions, you language-massacring bastards! You say 'I love it!'"

A man in his forties inside McDonald's gives the couple the finger before returning to the paper in front of him and taking a sip of coffee. All the diners start eating again, ignoring the couple, who are still shouting and banging on the window. It's only when an employee comes along brandishing a broom as though they were two stubborn pigeons that the couple moves on. Though not before the guy has made a peace sign at everyone and no one in particular.

Commercial Drive is long and wide. Apart from the out-of-place McDonald's, vegan restaurants jostle for space with homeopathic shops, and the people are a heady mix of ethnicities. The sky is just as gray as yesterday. My jet lag is still making me feel ill, as though my body is being pressed in from all sides by invisible forces.

When I can no longer see the hippy couple, I head in the direction where 1348 should be. In front of me a guy picks up a whole cigarette from the pavement. He turns to me and holds up his lucky find.

"A smoke!" he says. "I was walking along hoping for cigarettes and I found one!"

He closes his eyes and starts to pray.

"A hundred dollars, a hundred dollars," he mutters.

"Good luck," I say, smiling.

I walk on down the street. At 1302 is an acupuncture clinic that also sells Chinese medicine. In the shop sits an old Asian woman in a white lab coat, staring into space. The next few doors lead to apartment buildings. Most of them have different colored doors and in one of the windows there's a sign with a Ken Kesey quote: "You're either on the bus or off the bus."

At 1324 is a bookshop specializing in LGBT books. My heart starts to quicken. Suddenly I catch sight of the black canopy I saw on Google Street View. As I get closer I see that the name Caffé Amici has been painted over but that the place is still a café. I wonder how old the Google photo actually is. Since it's still several months until the summer, the trees aren't green of course, and the houses look a lot more dilapidated than in the photo.

My heart is beating like a percussion section now. I get to number 1348. It's a dry cleaner's that's closed down. On the wall outside there's a public telephone with the name Bell on a sign above it. I walk up to it. The receiver is hanging down and there are large burn marks around the numbers. Every surface is covered with graffiti and something I don't want to look at too closely has been smeared on the buttons. I hang the receiver back up gingerly.

For several minutes I stand there by the telephone. In the image online there was no dry-cleaner's and no phone box, and now it all seems so obvious. Part of me probably knew that I would never find Ben at 1348 Commercial Drive and that the whole thing was just a crazy, unrealistic dream. Clutching at straws. For the first time it strikes me like a punch in the stomach that I'm never going to see him again.

And that I'm never going to find out why he disappeared. Something breaks inside of me. I want to shout: "WHERE ARE YOU?! WHY DID YOU LIE TO ME? YOU SAID I WAS STUCK WITH YOU FOR THE REST OF MY LIFE!"

My legs can't hold me anymore, and I sink down under the telephone and fold myself into a little ball. The people who pass by ignore me. I'm just a wreck on Commercial Drive.

34

The hours that follow are hazy. On heavy legs I make my way back to the hotel. But on the train I change my mind, get off at some random station and start wandering around aimlessly. Nothing matters anymore. I drift around for several hours and end up suddenly back at the Buchanan.

Over the next three days, I only leave the hotel room to buy food. I cry, sleep, watch TV, sleep, cry, stare at the chintz curtains, eat food that doesn't have to be heated up, and cry a little more. On the fourth day, my fifth in Vancouver, I can't cry any more. I can't eat crackers and hummus any more. With relief and surprise, I also realize I'm over my jet lag, and that a restlessness has started to creep into my body. It's seven days until my flight back to Vienna.

Down in reception I ask if I can get an extra blanket, because I was cold the night before.

"Of course," the man at the desk says. "In case you're interested, a group from the hotel here are going out whale-watching today."

I don't answer at first. The thought of spending time with

other people, let alone strangers, feels exhausting to say the least. Being forced to engage in the kind of small talk I normally get paid for as a teacher. At the same time, I would actually like to see a whale.

"OK," I surprise myself by saying.

The group from the hotel consists of me, an Australian couple named Dave and Lee, and a Dutch woman with dreadlocks named Cornelia. After precise instructions from the man at reception, we bundle ourselves up in several layers of clothing and then take a local bus for over an hour. Dave, Lee, and Cornelia chat excitedly, while I sit quietly. A threadbare sock-puppet would probably be more interesting and appealing than I feel at the moment. But I still don't have any desire to take part in their backpacking tales, which seem to consist mainly of comparing the places they've been.

"So have you mostly travelled in Asia?" Lee asks Cornelia.

Cornelia nods. "Vietnam," she says. "And Cambodia."

"Cool," Lee says. "We've done Vietnam too."

"Isn't it fantastic?" Cornelia says.

"Totally," Lee says.

"Such a magical country," Cornelia says.

"Totally," Lee says.

Dave has started to flick through his camera, and I fear the worst. That he's trying to find the photos from their Vietnam trip.

"I've never met such fantastic people as in Vietnam," Cornelia goes on.

"Totally," Lee says.

"They were just so *genuine*."

I stare even harder out of the window at the suburbs we're

emmy abrahamson

passing in an attempt to block out their chatter and to stop myself giving Lee a dozen synonyms for "totally."

At some point, the trio start to discuss Canadian money.

"We've had plastic notes in Australia for almost twenty years," Dave says. "It's only now that the rest of the world is following our lead."

"They feel so weird," Cornelia says, carefully fingering a light-brown Canadian 100-dollar note. "Compared with the euro, I mean. So artificial and plasticky."

Dave takes the note from her.

"Did you know you can't rip them in half?" he says.

Then he rips it in two.

For a few seconds everyone stares at him. Dave's face turns as pale as a corpse and Lee bursts out laughing.

"Oh God! Oh God!" Dave cries. "I'm so sorry. They're supposed to be impossible to tear. Here, have one of mine."

He quickly gives Cornelia a 100-dollar note from his own wallet. I turn my head back towards the window, even though I can't help but smile.

We come to a place consisting of souvenir shops disguised as little fishing huts, which all have names starting with the word "captain" spelled "Capt'n." We pay for the tour and listen to a ten-minute long presentation about general boat etiquette and what we *might*—the group leader can't make any guarantees—see. Several times I see Dave and Lee exchange grins, making me feel like a very lonely little sock-puppet. One now wearing a red life jacket.

We steer out past the skerries and small islands, making our way into open waters. I sit in my life jacket, wishing with my whole body that Ben were beside me. What's the point of having experiences if you don't have anyone to say "Do you remember when . . . " to? Then I spot a bald eagle on a skerry. It's sitting on the branch of a fallen tree and I seem to be the only one who's seen it. The eagle is so still that I almost start believing that it is a fake put there by the tourist office, but then it cocks its head a little to the left. The other people in the boat catch sight of it and start taking pictures. I savor the moment when it was just me and the eagle.

The air is cold, and I have to bury my hands between my legs to stop them getting too chilly. We pass luxurious houses out by the coast. Some are built completely from wood, but others look like futuristic concrete cubes. By this point, most of the noses on the boat are red from the cold. When the clouds part there's a mass searching for sunglasses in bags.

"Now we are technically in American waters," the group leader says.

A woman looks down into the water immediately. If Ben had been here we would have tried to guess what she was looking for. Instead I see three seals diving down into the water. The group leader starts to get a little nervous that we haven't seen any whales yet and he says something to the man with the mustache and sunglasses who's driving the boat. The man just shrugs his shoulders.

"Over there!" someone cries suddenly.

I turn and gasp—about a hundred feet away is a group of killer whales. The man with the mustache and sunglasses turns off the engine and the whole boat falls silent. No one dares move. Black fins of different sizes roll soundlessly up and down across the surface of the water. The largest swims a little farther away. A six-foot-long dorsal fin and a coal-black back that seems never-ending cleave the water. We hear the sound of rushing air as several of the killer whales open their blowholes to breathe.

At a respectful distance, the boat begins to follow the pod of whales. It gets even colder. Suddenly we hear a loud splash and everyone in the boat turns the other way. Behind us, two killer whales have started to leap up out of the water. Almost all of their black and white bodies can be seen when they shoot, straight as arrows, out of the water before twisting and falling back down again. A third killer whale leaps up and flicks its tail fins before disappearing again in a cascade of water.

"They're playful today," the group leader says.

Around me cameras are clicking and now and then the group bursts out in jubilant cries.

"Pretty special, right?" Cornelia says, smiling at me.

It's only then that I realize my cheeks are covered with tears.

35

On the bus back to Vancouver, everyone is quiet. Thankfully even Total-Lee seems to understand that the experience we've shared would be spoiled by too much chatting. After a bit, Lee falls asleep against Dave's shoulder while he goes through the pictures on his camera.

When we're almost back at the hotel, I hear Dave, Lee, and Cornelia planning a camping trip and wondering where they should go. I immediately realize what an opportunity this is.

"Can I come with you?" I say suddenly. "I know a fantastic place."

A long silence follows, during which I age by about five years.

"Of course you can," Cornelia says at last.

"Do you have a tent?" Lee asks.

I shake my head.

"She can share with me," Cornelia says. "I've got a two-man tent."

"Do you have a sleeping bag?" Dave asks.

"No," I reply. "But I can buy one."

"The man at reception recommended Diamond Lake Park, near Okanagan Lake," Dave says.

"No," I say quickly. "Bouleau Lake. It's much better. Definitely Bouleau Lake. You won't regret it. It's amazing there."

"So have you been there before?" Dave asks. "I'd thought you'd never been to Canada?"

"As an adult, I meant," I say. "I've never been here *as an adult*. I was a totally different person then."

"A totally different person?" Lee repeats. "Were you born a boy?"

"No. I just mean that people are really different as children. Or teenagers," I say, a little irritated. "For example, I'm not ready to lay down my life for Kevin in the Backstreet Boys anymore. Anyway, Bouleau Lake is absolutely amazing."

Dave doesn't look completely convinced, but we decide to head there at eleven o'clock the next day anyway.

When I get back to my hotel room, my heart is pounding with nerves and excitement. *I'm going to Bouleau Lake!* Bouleau Lake, where I know Ben has been many times. Because I don't have a driver's license, I would never have been able to get there on my own. Perhaps there's a small chance there'll be something—anything that can help me track him down there. Then another thought hits me: *I'm going camping.*

I've never been camping before. I'm an indoor person. Nothing makes me more nervous than a sunny, cloudless day, because I know I should be outside, doing the kind of things outdoorsy people do (taking a measured sip from a robust flask; looking at a compass before staring at the horizon; talking about how it's "a whole other world out there"). In my dreams it's always raining. The closest I've come to being a nature person was when I hiked with Rebecca and Jesus-Jakob in the Lainzer Tiergarten one time. I tried to impress them with my knowledge of nature but almost managed to kill Jesus-Jakob by mistaking lily-of-the-valley for wild garlic. And now I'm going to camp.

At quarter to eleven the next day, everyone's ready to leave. Dave has rented a four-wheel drive and we're stuffing in tents, sleeping bags, backpacks (theirs), suitcases (mine), and bags of shopping and camping equipment. As compensation for having invited myself I've insisted on buying the food and, via Cornelia, I've borrowed a sleeping bag from an Italian girl on the fourth floor. Dave and Lee sit in the front of the car, and Cornelia and I are in the back. Dave carefully enters our destination into the GPS.

"Are we nearly there yet?" I say as soon as Dave pulls out onto the road from the hotel.

Cornelia giggles and says: "I need the bathroom."

"If you two don't pipe down you won't get any more lollies," Lee says from the front seat.

Cornelia and I look at one another. We stay quiet for ten seconds.

"Are we there yet?" we cry in unison.

"Bloody kids," Dave mutters.

~

On the way there, my nerves increase because you never know with Ben. *What if Bouleau Lake is a radioactive dumping ground? Or it's closed to the public? And what am I actually hoping to find here?*

Three hours later we're almost there. We've driven through snow-topped mountains and desert landscapes. Unfortunately we've also seen mile after mile of brown, dry, dead forests. Victims of the mass-murdering pine beetle. At several points, there are still snowdrifts. Lee gets annoyed when she realizes Cornelia and I have eaten all the strawberry Twizzlers, but aside from that we've had a fun road trip. I've found out that Dave and Lee are not only engaged but also second cousins, and that Cornelia owns an organic clothing store in Rotterdam.

"It looks pretty wild," Cornelia says, as we turn off the main road and start following the signs to Bouleau Lake. "Was it like this the last time you were here?"

"Absolutely," I say, with as much conviction as I can.

The road is so uneven we have to hold on, and we drive through wilderness for over twenty minutes. The road doesn't appear to have been used for a while, and for a good distance the car climbs a steep slope above a little stream.

"Did you see that rusty car down there?" I say with some unease.

But I'm the only one who did. Half of the car was covered with undergrowth and in my head I can even see four skeletons sitting inside it. With their seatbelts on and empty Twizzlers packets beside them.

Dave has to concentrate so hard on driving that he's stopped talking.

Suddenly we turn onto an open area beside a lake. We've arrived.

"Wow," I cry.

The water glitters in the sun, and all around us, thank

God, are nothing but green forests. Dave gets out and looks at something on the front of the car. I stretch my legs and look around me, relieved that it really is a beautiful place. The camping ground contains three campfire sites. The air is cold and bracing. To the west lies the lake and on all the other three sides we're surrounded by forest. There's an arrow-shaped "Toilet" sign nailed to a tree. We're the only people at the campsite. And Ben's not here. Of course. Nor are there any ants forming an arrow pointing in the direction he disappeared in. Of course. Still, I'm glad to be at a place I know he liked so much.

The more experienced campers immediately start putting up the tents. I take a metal peg and start pushing it into the ground where Cornelia is spreading out her tent.

"What are you doing?" Cornelia asks.

"Putting the tent up," I reply, somewhat uncertainly.

"That stake goes in the corner. I thought you'd been camping before?"

"Tents in Sweden are different. Not as many pegs," I say, gesturing to the equipment.

"It's OK," Cornelia says. "I've done it so many times I'll be quicker doing it myself."

Relieved to have gotten out of helping, I go and test the cold water. It's like dipping your hand into an ice-fishing hole. A little farther out on the lake I can see some people paddling a canoe. They must have set up camp in another site. They wave at me. I wave at them. They wave at me again. I wave at them again. *So this is the camping life*, I think, as a little lump of metal melts inside my city-girl heart.

Lee and I go on a hunt for dry branches. In the sun it's

warm enough to walk without a jacket, although the temperature seems to dip drastically in the shade.

"This is so cool," I say excitedly.

"What?" Lee asks.

I wave at the forest around us.

"This," I say. "Looking for branches!"

Lee just looks at me.

"OK," she says after a pause.

Lee is quite obviously the wrong person to share my branch-hunting excitement with.

A few hours later the campfire is burning and we are cooking food. By "we" I mean Dave. Lee, Cornelia, and I are the cheerleaders. We eat baked potatoes and corn on the cob that have been buried next to the fire, and sausages. Dave and Lee have already drunk several beers, while Cornelia and I are sharing a bottle of wine. After so many years in Vienna I was mildly alarmed at the price of alcohol in Canada, and because I didn't recognize any of the wines I chose the one with the prettiest label.

It starts to get dark. Apart from the odd bird, the forest around us is quiet, and the only sound is the crackle of the fire.

"The great outdoors isn't so bad after all," I say, looking out across the lake.

"Right?" Cornelia says.

Dave comes back from the toilet. He hasn't zipped up his fly yet.

"I heard something that could have been a bear," he says, exhilarated.

"That's only because you're *hoping* we're going to see a bear," Lee says.

"I'll be keeping my knife on hand anyway," Dave says, taking it out of a leather sheath on his belt.

Cornelia starts digging around in her backpack.

"And I have a whistle," she says, holding it up.

"And I can scare it off with an explanation of the difference between transitive and intransitive verbs," I say.

"That'll do the trick." Dave says, putting his knife away.

We open another bottle of wine and toast marshmallows. The conversation turns to misunderstood song lyrics. I tell them how I thought for years that Bob Marley was singing "No woman, no crime," while Cornelia says she always thought Robert Palmer was singing "Might as well face it, you're a dick with a glove."

"My English wasn't great back then. But of course I knew all the swear words," she says in her defense. "And I never saw the title of the song. So for years I thought 'dick with a glove' was just some English term for idiots. Because Michael Jackson only wore one glove."

"What would Robert Palmer have had against Michael Jackson?" Lee asks.

"That was what I never understood!" Cornelia says, shaking her dreadlocks.

I laugh so much I have tears in my eyes. It's now completely dark, but in the glow of the fire I can almost see Ben sitting beside us. He looks at me and grins. And I know what he would be thinking. *Finally.* I make up my mind to knock on Elfriede Jelinek's door as soon as I get back to Vienna and tell her how much I admire her, and I'm going to start singing in a choir and traveling more. These thoughts make me so happy, and because Ben has in some way brought me to these decisions, I decide to finally tell everyone the reason I'm here.

"Do you want to know why I actually came to Canada?" I say, and everyone nods. So I tell the whole story of Ben and me to Lee, Dave, and Cornelia. But when I'm done I don't get the reaction I'd been hoping for. No one says what a romantic gesture it is, or that of course I'm going to find him. Instead everyone looks a little bit embarrassed and they don't say anything at all.

"He really didn't leave a single message?" Lee asks at last.

I shake my head.

Cornelia shrugs. "A good fuck is worth fighting for," she says in the no-nonsense way only Dutch women with dreads can.

36

A zebra-striped van pulls up out of nowhere. For a long time we just stare at this black-and-white apparition. No one gets out. After thirty seconds, the side door opens and two guys climb out. One of them has the most impressive mullet I've ever seen. The hair on top is so short it stands up in little shiny spikes, before turning into a softly flowing mane at his neck.

"Hey!" the Mullet says.

"Hey!" Dave replies.

The Mullet and his friend, who is a little shorter, come over to us.

"Is it OK if we sit with you?" Mullet asks. "It's too late to start our own fire."

"Of course," Dave says.

"We were thinking of going to bed soon," Lee says, and gives Dave a meaningful glance.

Mullet points at himself. "I'm Duffy. This is my bro, Adam."

Adam lifts his hand.

"I'm Dave and this is Lee."

"Julia," I say.

"Cornelia," says Cornelia.

It's only now that I realize both Duffy the Mullet and Adam are swaying. Which makes me wonder who was driving. Suddenly, a third guy gets out of the van like a surprise number at a Russian circus. Duffy and Adam start to applaud.

"Pickle! You're awake!" Duffy says, before turning to us again. "This is Pickled Mike. His wife left him today."

Pickled Mike rubs his eyes and sits down with a bump by the fire. Adam goes over to the van and comes back with a torn brown paper bag. He starts passing beers to everyone who wants one from the bag. I decide to stick to the wine.

"Why are you called Pickled Mike?" I ask.

"Fucked if I know," Pickled Mike answers, opening a beer.

"So are you here to fish?" Duffy asks.

He's the only one who's not sitting down. Instead, he's standing, legs apart, looking us over.

"Nah," Dave replies. "Just camping."

"Two tents," Duffy says, nodding at the tents.

Since it's unclear whether this is a question or an observation, no one replies. Pickled Mike suddenly gets up and disappears into the van. He slams the door behind him.

"His wife left him today," Duffy says.

"You said," Dave says.

"Fucking bitch," Duffy says.

The new campers have changed the mood around the fire and none of us knows quite how we should behave. I notice Adam staring at me and Cornelia. Duffy picks up a half-eaten corn on the cob from the paper plate beside Lee.

"Is it OK if I eat this?" he asks.

"Sure," Lee says with a smile that's not really a smile.

Duffy starts gnawing on the corn. Adam is still staring at me and Cornelia. In the end he looks at us and smiles.

"So are you . . . you know . . ." he begins.

"From Europe?" I finish for him. "Yes."

Adam starts to giggle.

"No," he says. "Are you . . . ?"

Once again he leaves the rest of the question hanging.

"Members of yakuza?" I say. "No."

Adam giggles even harder. "No."

"Lovers of good food?" I say. "Yes. To be quite honest, if you don't finish your question we could go on like this all night."

"Are you . . . you know . . . together?"

Duffy immediately turns his attention to us.

"Lesbians! Are! Hot!" he shouts. "Gays make me puke, but lesbos . . ." He smacks his lips. "Come to Daddy!"

"We're not together," I say. "And we're straight."

Only an hour earlier, Cornelia told us that she is married to a man from Senegal who's fifteen years younger than her, but that they are going to get divorced because his hash habit is so bad they've stopped having sex. But Adam carries on smiling as though he doesn't believe me. At that moment, the door to the van slides open again and out jumps Pickled Mike. With a big grin and a guitar.

"Oh, fuck," Duffy mutters. "He's got the guitar."

Pickled Mike sits by the fire again and for the first time he looks at us all.

"Johnny Cash got arrested for picking flowers," he says, and starts playing the guitar.

Duffy goes over and lifts up the brown paper bag.

"What the fuck, Adam!" he yells and wads up the bag.

"What the fuck, Duffy!" Adam retorts.

Pickled Mike carries on playing, and sings something softly.

Duffy points at Adam and turns to us. "Do you know what his job is?" he says. "Guess. Guess."

We shake our heads.

"He's a cook at an old folks' home," Duffy says with a snort.

"At least I have a job," Adam says. "Instead . . ."

"I'm a professional fucking snowboarder," Duffy interrupts.

"*Were*," Adam corrects him. " . . . instead of making my haircut my career."

Duffy's face immediately turns beetroot red, and he hurls himself at his brother. Dave, Lee, Cornelia, and I leap up and take several steps backwards. Duffy and Adam fight so violently that they're rolling around on the floor, beating each other with hard punches. They're both groaning from the pain and the effort. By the fire, Pickled Mike goes on playing his guitar.

37

I'm the first one to react.

"Stop! Stop!" I shout. "Dave, help me!"

Dave and I run over and try to pull the fighting pair apart. It's pretty easy, which makes me think it was probably more of a performance by the two brothers than anything else.

"Asshole," Adam mutters.

"Asshole," Duffy replies.

Everyone sits back down around the fire and there's a short silence. The only thing that can be heard is Pickled Mike's guitar and muffled singing. To lighten the mood I ask the trio if they'd like some wine. They all say yes, and Adam gets some old paper cups from the van. Pickled Mike picks an old cigarette butt out of his before pouring the wine.

"I had a real mug in the van once, which I stole from Starbucks," Adam says. "But then someone took it at a gas station. How fucking low can you sink?"

"So, are you allowed to get married in your countries?" Duffy asks after taking a gulp.

"We're not together," Cornelia says. "But yeah, in the

Netherlands homosexuals can get married. And in Sweden too, where Julia is from."

Pickled Mike stares at us immediately.

"Are you a couple?" he says. "Cool! Good for you!"

Suddenly he rushes into the van and closes the door.

Duffy stares after him.

"Tight bastard," he mutters. "He doesn't want to share his coke with anyone. Right now he's probably sniffing his twentieth line without offering it to anyone. If his wife hadn't left him today I probably would have beaten him up for that."

"Why did she leave him?" I ask.

"Who knows? She was always damn weird," Duffy says. "She was like forty-two when they got married and Pickle was twenty-five. She had a serious job and everything. In a bank. And wore real clothes when she went to work. But then she was hanging out with this group of guys in their twenties when she wasn't working. She had like no friends her own age. What kind of woman has no friends of her own when she's over forty?"

"A fucking weird one," Adam interjects.

"We always thought it was annoying that she hung out with us but we never said anything because Pickle was so happy. If anyone should have left anyone, it should have been *him* leaving *her*."

The van door slides open again and Pickled Mike jumps out. He's bare-chested and his eyes are larger than when we last saw him. He beats himself on the chest several times, like a male gorilla.

"Pickle!" Adam cheers. "Pickle! Pickle! Pickle!"

Pickled Mike points at Adam and grins. "You speak the truth, my friend," he says.

Then he turns to me and Cornelia. "If you want to make out, you can just start whenever you like," he says.

This talk about Cornelia and me being together is getting a little old. I'm happy for the Canadian Marx brothers to carry on the night without me so I stand up to go to bed. I also need to pee. When I get up and everything sways a little I realize I've drunk more than I thought.

"Are you going to bed?" Cornelia asks.

I nod.

"In that case I'll come soon too," she says.

I notice Adam, Duffy, and Pickled Mike exchanging knowing smirks.

It would be a suicide mission to try to find the toilet in the dark, so I make for the nearest bush among the trees behind my and Cornelia's tent. Just a few meters away from the fire it's so cold I'm shivering. I pull my trousers and pants down and hold on tight to a branch so I don't fall backwards. For a long time nothing happens—my body doesn't seem to want to pee in protest against the cold.

The smell. Before my brain has even had time to understand, my body has already registered the smell that hits me like a wave. It's sweet, like dry grass mixed with urine. I look up and see the bear less than five meters away from me. I hear its wet breathing and suddenly I have no problem peeing. Even though I read in the Lonely Planet guide about what you should do if you meet a bear, I can't remember a thing now. Surprise turns to fear. The bear's eyes are uncannily indifferent and at the same time determined, and now I'm unsure whether the deep breathing is coming from me or the bear. Or both. The smell. *What a unique, animal smell*, is my only—

ridiculously obvious—thought. Suddenly the bear stands up on its hind legs. Its fur looks dusty and hangs slack—as though it were three sizes too big. The bear makes a kind of sneezing noise and opens its mouth. I know that's not a good sign. I don't want to die in Canada. Torn to shreds by a bear with my butt exposed. My hope has always been to die after a really nice nap in a meadow somewhere. A branch snaps. Both the bear and I turn to see what it is. It's Pickled Mike. In the glow from the fire he stands bare-chested, glaring furiously at the bear.

"LEAVE THE SWISS GIRL ALONE!" he roars.

And with that, he takes three strides forwards and gives the bear a right jab on the nose. The world stands still, and for a few seconds Pickled Mike and the bear just stare at each other. Then the bear turns and disappears among the trees. There's the sound of branches and twigs breaking under its hasty retreat.

38

Pickled Mike raises his right arm and jogs in small circles, humming "Gonna Fly Now," the theme tune from *Rocky*. I'm still maintaining my vice-like grip on the branch with my pants round my knees, but finally, with great effort, I'm able to let it go.

At last I manage to stand and pull up my pants, but my hands are shaking so much I can't do the zipper. I feel like something's pressing on my ribcage, and my skin is burning up. By this point the others have come over to see what's going on.

"What the hell?" Duffy asks.

"A bear. But I showed him who Mr. Miyagi was," says Pickled Mike, boxing the air in a confusion of early eighties films.

My body is trembling so much Cornelia has to support me until we get back to the fire.

"I missed it," Dave says, looking dejectedly at the forest.

"How you doing?" Lee asks.

I shake my head.

"I can't believe I was nearly attacked by a grizzly bear," I say.

"Black bear," Pickled Mike corrects me.

"Aha," I say, a little disappointed. I decide that in future retellings the bear will be a grizzly anyway.

"If it had been a grizzly, you wouldn't be sitting here now," Duffy says.

"Shouldn't we leave here?" Lee asks. "What if it comes back?"

Adam and Duffy sit down by the fire again.

"It's not coming back," Adam says. "It won't want to have anything to do with us and we certainly don't want to have anything to do with it."

"But how can you be so sure?"

"It's *not* coming back," Duffy repeats.

"But how can you be so sure?" Lee repeats.

Duffy gives Lee a long look.

"If I'd punched you in the kisser, you think you'd be coming back? Bears aren't unforgiving Ninja Turtles. It hasn't gone away to plan its revenge. Do you have many animals out for revenge where you live? Kangaroos crafting cunning plans?"

Lee doesn't respond.

Adam makes his eyes large and puffs his face up. "I'm a koala and I'm going to settle the score," he says in a reedy voice. "But first I'm going to eat some eucalyptus. Slowly."

Adam, Duffy, and Pickled Mike are laughing so much they're on the floor as they go on doing impressions of Australian animals desperate for vengeance.

"Is there any more wine?" Duffy says at last, drying his eyes and stretching his legs out.

The next morning I count seventy-two blackfly bites on my legs from the previous night, even though I was wearing long pants the whole time.

When I get out of the tent I see that Adam's already up and the fire's lit. Long shadows fall across the campsite, and the ground is still frozen. Adam smiles at me.

"Pickle's caught some trout," he says.

On the log by the fire, three fish lie in a neat row.

"When did he catch them?" I ask. I pull my jacket even tighter around me.

"This morning," Adam says. "And I'm making eggs Benedict."

There are some English muffins grilling over the fire, and Adam's whisking up some hollandaise sauce in a pan. When I look around the campsite I notice that Adam, Duffy, and Pickled Mike have also cleaned up all our trash. From the door of the zebra-striped van, Duffy waves to me as he sits and smokes. He must have been swimming, because his mullet is damp, hanging in corkscrew curls.

"I heard some animals during the night," I say. "Howling."

"Could have been prairie dogs," Adam says.

"Or wolves," Duffy says from the van, waving away an insect.

We all eat breakfast. Pickled Mike, Adam, and Duffy ask us perfectly normal questions and give us advice about places we ought to see on the way back to Vancouver. I know it's a long shot, but I ask anyway.

"Do you know Ben? He likes to come up here too."

"You mean Short-No-Hair-Limp-Dick-Ben?" Duffy asks.

"Nah, he's tall. Very tall. With dark, slightly curly hair."

Adam looks at Duffy. "Maybe she means Benny?"

"Benny moved to Manitoba," Duffy says. "And had himself sterilized."

"Big Ben, then? But he's going bald."

"And is dead. Don't you remember—he crashed his car and died a year ago?"

"Shit! I'd forgotten about that. And what was his brother's name . . ."

While they carry on talking I start packing up our things.

39

Dave and Lee have gone back to Australia, and Cornelia has gone on to Seattle. We've all resolved to stay in touch, and Cornelia has promised to come to Vienna and visit me. I already miss her dry sense of humor and Lee and Dave's relaxed attitude to life. I didn't manage to find Ben, didn't even come close, but at least I can boast about knowing someone in Wonglepong, Queensland. And even though I disagreed with Ben that time on Donauinsel and insisted that you can't make new friends after a certain age, that is exactly what I've done, and I'm glad.

There's three days left until I head back to Vienna. Like a lonesome but ambitious little cloud I do a sightseeing bus trip, eat dim sum in Chinatown, and stare at a squid in the Stanley Park aquarium. I go to a café and order a "raspberry cordial soda," but they have no idea what I'm talking about so I have a coffee instead.

On the way to the anthropological museum, I notice it's close to Wreck Beach, which Ben had mentioned but I'd completely forgotten about. Since it's the first cloudless day in

Vancouver, I decide to go there first. When we get to the bus stop I ask the driver which way Wreck Beach is.

"Over there," he says, pointing towards some woods. "Then you take the steps down. Sure you won't be cold?"

He laughs.

Since I'm bundled up with a scarf and gloves I shake my head and then can't figure out why he's still chuckling to himself.

Through the forest I follow some winding steps down. Sometimes it's so steep I have to hold the railing, and sometimes there are pleasant short gaps between the steps. Tall Douglas firs surround the track. The steps never seem to end, and I read on a sign that there are 483 of them. Finally I come out of the forest and down onto the sand. A brisk wind is blowing on the shore.

"Hello," a voice says. "How are you?"

A man in his seventies walks past me. Apart from a neon-green fanny pack around his waist and sandals on his feet, he's naked.

"Gr . . . er . . ." I manage to say, staring at his shriveled behind.

Including the old man and me, there are seven people on the beach. Six of them aren't wearing any clothes. I almost start laughing. Of course Ben's favorite beach would be a nudist beach.

I go down towards the water and sit on the stones to gaze at the view. To enjoy it like Ben said he'd enjoyed himself here. Across the water I can see houses, and behind them the snow-topped North Shore Mountains. The air on Wreck Beach smells of salt and seaweed, with a weak note of marijuana which makes me think of Matthias, and I wonder why we were together so long. Why I believed that love had to be such a struggle. Why I thought it was normal to "work" at a relationship as though it was a shift in a Russian uranium mine. With Ben, everything was so easy, so natural, so self-explanatory. Until he disappeared and everything fell apart.

I look at the guy with the fanny pack. He's sitting on a towel a little way away. The sun has gone behind a cloud for a moment, but he's strung up a little purple tie-dye canopy, which he's sitting under. I get up and walk over to him.

"Excuse me," I say. "I wonder if I could ask you something?"

The guy smiles. His cheeks and chin are covered with rough-looking white stubble.

"Of course," he says. "What is it you want to know?"

I do everything I can to stop my gaze drifting down to his penis, which calls to mind a gloomy little sausage between the bit of white pubes and wrinkled testicles. The beach is not warm.

"I wonder if you've ever seen a guy called Ben here at Wreck Beach?" I say. "He's very tall. And he has dark hair. Perhaps a beard sometimes. He's . . . lively."

The guy laughs. "Of course I know Ben," he says.

I suddenly find it hard to breathe, and my body wants to crumple.

"Everyone knows Benjy-Benito," the old guy goes on. "He used to entertain us every summer. Along with his buddies. He was a really cool guy. We shared a joint now and then."

I hardly dare ask the next question.

"Have you seen him lately? Over the last few months maybe?"

The guy shakes his head and scratches at the white hair on his chest. His nails are long and yellow.

"Nah, I haven't seen him for a few years. From what I heard he'd moved to T.O."

The guy carries on scratching himself. It makes a dry scraping sound.

"T.O.? What's that?"

"Toronto."

"Not Europe?"

The guy shakes his head.

No, the trail can't stop here.

He finally stops scratching his sunken ribcage. Instead he gets a pot of lip balm out of his fanny pack.

"Do you know anyone who might know more about him? Someone else I could talk to?" I ask.

"I know he used to go to Vito's on Commercial Drive," the guy says. "You can always ask there." He starts carefully applying the balm to his lips.

"You don't happen to know Ben's last name?"

"Nope. We always called him Ben, Benjy, or Benjy-Benito. Don't ask why. But he always made me laugh."

I thank the old guy and almost run back to the wooden steps. The whole way I curse myself for having forgotten about Wreck Beach. Stupidity can take many forms and right now it is taking the form of someone who has to stop several times to catch her breath on the way up.

40

I'm back on Commercial Drive, and it doesn't take long to find Vito's. It's a trashy bar with graffiti on the front wall that doesn't open for two hours. I wander around the grocery store next door and look at the products until the Vietnamese sales assistant starts looking at me weirdly. I listen to a girl with a center part playing electric guitar. My stomach starts growling with hunger, so I buy a piece of pizza with pesto on it from a place called Uncle Fatih's. I walk up and down in front of Vito's like a restless dog. At last I see a guy with dyed-black hair unlock the door before quickly slipping in and closing it. After ten minutes he opens the door again and starts taking off the wooden boards that adorn the barred windows. The guy has big black rings in his ears and a horseshoe barbell through his nose. Each eyebrow has at least three piercings.

"Excuse me," I begin.

"What?" he says. The guy stops and turns his full attention on me.

"I was wondering if you knew, or know, a guy called Ben

or Benjy or Benjy-Benito," I say. "He's tall and has dark hair."

The guy gives a little shrug.

"There must be a few Bens who come here. But we have too many customers for me to be able to remember anyone's name. Sorry."

The guy looks genuinely apologetic that he can't help me, which almost has me in tears.

"Are you sure? Ben?" I repeat. "He had a cousin who died."

"As I said, we have loads of customers every evening so who knows? He might come here. Sorry. Why are you looking for him?"

"No reason," I say. "I just want to say hello."

The guy looks at me and I notice that one of his eyebrow piercings is infected.

"I really wish I could help you," he says.

"Me too," I say, my voice trembling.

The guy seems suddenly to come to a decision and gets out his phone.

"Wait, I'll call Sherri," he says. "She has a better memory than me."

A minute later I've explained the situation to Sherri. As I'm speaking to her, the guy bends down, grabs hold of the wooden boards, and carries them in.

"I think I might be able to remember a guy like that," the voice at the other end of the line says a little tentatively. "And if I remember rightly that gang—him and his cousin and a few others—used to hang out at Donny's in Burnaby as well. I think they lived somewhere near there. Maybe you can check there?"

I thank Sherri and immediately ask the black-haired guy how to get to Donny's. When he explains I have to get the SkyTrain eastwards, I take off, almost at a run.

On the train I'm tense and impatient, and my legs keep jiggling up and down. I have so little time, and yet I feel like I'm so close to finding Ben, and that soon I'll be able to apologize for everything. I chew the inside of my cheek and look out of the window at the view, which is constantly switching between impoverished, tumbledown shacks, and richer, white-fronted houses and shops. A young woman sits down opposite me on the train. She has bottle-blonde hair, a pink Hello Kitty top, and black stone-washed jeans. I can't help noticing that one of her nipples is pierced, because the outline of the metal ring is bulging out through Kitty's left ear. When she starts looking for something in her bag I see her nails.

"Your nails," I burst out.

The girl smiles and holds them up.

"Cool, right?" she says.

She puts her hands out so I can get a closer look. On every one of her long fingernails there's a perfect little color photo of a smiling face, plus one of a dog.

"It's my mum, my stepdad, my little brother, my two half-sisters, three friends, and my dog. Though I regret doing *her*." She points at the nail on her left index finger, which is decorated with a girl with long dark hair. "We're not friends anymore because she turned out to be a cunt."

"It's like having a photo album on your nails," I say. "I didn't know you could even do something like that."

"It's really big right now. There's a place on Kingsway in Burnaby that does it," the girl says. "Can I see yours?"

"My what?"

"Nails," the girl says.

I show her my short unpainted nails a little self-consciously.

"They're nudists," I say.

The girl grins. "They should head over to Wreck Beach then."

"I've just been there," I say. "But it was a little cold."

Now I notice the girl has little plastic Disney characters as earrings. Goofy in her left ear and Minnie Mouse in the right.

"Wreck Beach is so fucking overrated anyway," she says, rolling her eyes. "All those steps and then there's just a load of stinking hippies with tits down to their waists and old guys with beer bellies. And the police out every evening checking no one's openly drinking alcohol. The last time I went, there was a guy lying there and staring at me and my friends while he jerked off. He got beaten up for it."

"Once, on the metro in Vienna where I live, this guy started jerking off a few seats away from me," I say. "When he saw that I'd noticed what he was doing he told me it wouldn't take long."

"As if that was going to make it better," the girl says.

"I know," I say, shaking my head.

"My name's Jordana," she says.

"Julia," I say.

The girl brightens. "Your name begins with J too—cool."

I smile back and wish my life was so simple that alliterating names were enough to make me happy. Jordana gets her phone out and in the reflection she applies pink lip gloss from a glittery tube. Even though she dresses like an eleven-year-old, I can see now that she must be over twenty-five.

"I'm going to meet a guy I really like," she says, while she carefully brushes away a speck of mascara from under one eye. "Gotta look good."

"Oh, nice," I say.

"He's a real catch," she says. "So I have to turn the speakers up to eleven if I'm going to snag him. If you know what I mean?"

"*This is Spinal Tap*," I say, smiling.

She stands up to go.

"Are you getting out here too?" she asks me.

"No . . . I think I'm getting off at the next stop."

"OK, well have a nice evening," she says.

"You too," I say, "and good luck."

I watch Jordana as she gets off the train and smile to myself a little. I've talked to a stranger on a train. Ben would have been proud.

I get off at the next station, but the black-haired guy must have been wrong, because I can't see anywhere called Donny's at all. When I ask a man who's walking past he tells me I should have got off at the previous stop. With no idea when the next train is coming, I start walking back.

The area is nice and feels a lot like a small town. The houses don't look that expensive, but they're all clean and well looked after. An elderly lady who's weeding her garden greets me, and I return the greeting.

I walk for several kilometers and get so warm I have to take off my scarf and carry it. I pass a motel that could be a set for an American film, right down to the broken neon writing, and then a bridge stretching across a river. On the other side there's a Tim Hortons, followed by a Starbucks and several cafés and shops. Everything looks at once impersonal and welcoming.

At last I see a rectangular white building with a black sign that says "Donny's." There's a parking lot in front of it that's almost completely empty. I stop for a few seconds to get my breath back and look up. The air is warm, and the sky has turned that pale lilac color it goes just before dusk. Then the door to Donny's opens and I see Jordana from the SkyTrain walk out. She puts an arm around the waist of the guy walking alongside her, and laughs at something he says. The guy. Ben.

41

I immediately duck behind a beige car. The pain inside me makes everything go black for a second and I have to steady myself against the dusty car door. *No, this can't be happening again.* History can't be repeating itself. Ben and Matthias. Matthias and Ben. Matthias sitting by the kitchen table telling me they'd been looking at Mamiya cameras in one of his lessons, even though he actually hadn't been at the photography school for months. Ben who told me I was stuck with him forever, and who's now with someone else. *Please no, not again.* My whole body is burning and I'm struggling to breathe. I never knew that feelings could lead to such physical pain. A woman walking past the car looks at me strangely, so I get up and start running back to the train. I run and run. I run past a gang of teenage girls who yell something I don't quite catch. I run past the Starbucks and the Tim Hortons.

I'm proud of myself for not crying on the train. I don't cry on the walk back to the hotel. I don't cry as I say hello to the man at reception and walk up the stairs at the hotel. I don't cry as I take off my clothes, shower, put my pajamas on, or brush my teeth. It's only when I've crept in between the bedside table and the bed, so that I'm completely hemmed in, that I allow the tears to flow.

42

It's Bettina, Steffi, and Hans's last lesson at Berlitz. Steffi gives me a box of Merci chocolates.

"Thanks," I say.

With claret-red cheeks, Bettina mumbles something and gives me a few stapled-together sheets of paper with photos on them. At first I don't understand what they are. But then I realize she's taken photos of her family and her two cats with a little caption in English under each one. On the last page there's a photo of Bettina holding up a long-stemmed glass of prosecco. Underneath, it says:

Dear Julia! You are the best teacher! Your lessons was my joy. You were very useful. Thank you! Bettina!

I give Bettina a long hug and try not to cry. Steffi looks annoyed that Bettina has given such a personal present. Hans looks at the photo of Bettina where she's raising the glass. Then he points at me.

"You've made Bettina . . . an alcohol . . ." he says, but then can't find the right word.

"I've made Bettina an *alcoholic*?" I go on. "I certainly hope so. As long as she can speak English."

Hans shakes my hand and my three former students disappear forever. Hans is the only one who's gotten a new job, while Bettina and Steffi will continue along the meandering paths of unemployment.

I look out of the window, which is streaked with dirt, to see if the much-longed-for rain is finally on its way, but the sky is still bright blue. There's a balled-up piece of paper and a couple of paper clips on the windowsill. Carefully, I put the box of chocolates and Bettina's collage into my bag.

There's no one duller than someone with a broken heart, so I've hidden myself away ever since I came back from Canada. I teach, go to the gym, watch my new life-partner (Netflix), read, and sleep. Since Canada I've been sleeping a lot. And when I'm not sleeping I'm mostly thinking about how nice it's going to be to sleep.

But today I decide to do something I should have done a long time ago: after work I go and buy an indoor azalea.

The heat of summer has emptied the streets of the city's native residents and replaced them with ice cream-eating tourists with tired eyes. It's so warm you can only move in slow motion. Happily, the houses in the seventh district are so tall that the sidewalks are kept pleasantly shaded, even though everything has become oppressively dusty again.

Full of purpose, I go to the second floor of my building and ring the doorbell of the flat that faces onto the street. Though part of me is hoping there'll be no one at home, I immediately see a shadow behind the frosted-glass door panes. Someone unbolts two locks and opens the door.

"*Grüss Gott*," I say. "And sorry to disturb you. My name is Julia and I live on the fourth floor. I just wanted to give you this and tell you how much I admire you."

I hold out the potted plant, which is wrapped in white paper and a curl of green ribbon. Elfriede Jelinek is short and looks very neat. Her eyes are made up and she's wearing a soft red lipstick.

"Thank you," she says and looks happy and surprised.

Then she closes the door.

I stand there like an idiot. Did she misunderstand my German and think I was a courier delivering the plant? Didn't she realize that the whole point was for her to invite me into her flat so we could become friends? We wouldn't even need to become friends, but during our conversation she was supposed to at least tell me something about being an author or about life, or about the men who would change my life.

Disturbed by the woman's heartlessness I almost ring the doorbell again, to force her to say something insightful. But then I hear someone come in through the door from the street, so I leave the cold-hearted Jelinek's door and start going up to my own apartment.

As I'm going up the stairs I have a flash of inspiration and suddenly realize what I'm going to write about. It's all so obvious; Elfriede has helped me in spite of everything. My book is going to be about an English teacher who's sitting on a bench on Karlsplatz one day when a stranger suddenly sits down next to her. And everything changes forever.

As soon as I enter my apartment I know something is not quite right. Firstly, Optimus isn't sitting waiting for me on the mat in the hall, and secondly, the apartment smells different. I walk into the bedroom and stop short. Ben is asleep in the bed.

43

I stand beside the bed staring at him for a long time. I notice he's cut his hair and put on a little weight since I saw him in Canada. I spot the backpack that's leaning against the wall and the damp towel that's been thrown over the bedroom door.

"Ben," I say.

He doesn't move.

"Ben," I say, a little louder.

He opens his eyes.

"Hi," he says, smiling.

He shifts up against the wall.

"My flight to Bratislava was delayed," he says with a yawn. "And then I had to sleep on the floor of the airport until the buses to Vienna started running. But then my bus had some problem with its engine, so everyone had to get off and wait for a replacement one."

I'm standing completely still. Ben throws off the cover.

"Come here," he says with a smile. "God, I've missed you."

"Get out," I say.

I see fear in his eyes.

"Get out of my flat," I repeat. "I'm *not* going to do this. Pretend that the last few months never happened. Get out! Get out of my flat and out of my life."

Ben sits up.

"I tried to call you," he says nervously. "Several times. You never answered."

"You tried once," I say.

He appears to give this some thought.

"I'm sure I called more than once."

"*I'm* sure you didn't."

When I look at Ben the pain comes back; the pain I've been so good at suppressing since Canada.

"Why did you leave me?" I ask. "Was it because of that fight?"

He doesn't reply.

"Was it because of that fight?" I repeat, my voice rising.

"Yes! At least, at first it was," Ben said. "Of course I was angry at the things you said, who wouldn't be? So I stayed at Pawel's from work for a while. Before I headed back to Canada."

"And how did you get the money for that? By plastering walls?"

"Of course not," he hisses. "My dad lent it to me. And not without a struggle I might add. But I've paid him back."

"I thought you were dead!" I scream. "Or in prison. Or in the hospital. Or whatever!"

"I took off to Canada for your sake!" Ben says. "For you!"

I wait for him to continue.

"You have no idea what it's like to have no money," he

goes on. "To be in one of the world's most beautiful cities and not be able to afford anything. I went to Canada to earn money. For us. You've seen the kind of shitty jobs I'm able to get here in Vienna. Like being a Mozart clown or working for Poles who don't even pay you half the time."

"But that's your own fault!" I say. "It was your decision to hitch from one country to another. It was your choice not to do anything with your life. And are there really such fantastic, well-paid jobs in Canada?"

"At least there are jobs where I can earn a lot of money fast," Ben says. "I was so fucking sick of you paying for everything."

I'm so angry I can hardly breathe.

"How fucking *dare* you guilt-trip me for working and earning money!" I say. "I'm ever so sorry for spending money on you and wanting to have fun with you, but fun things *cost money*! The only reason it stings is that I'm a woman, right? But you know what? *I* didn't mind. Why couldn't you even get in touch with me or leave me a tiny little message when you were in Canada? That's not how normal people behave! That's how assholes behave!"

Ben makes a frustrated gesture with his hands and points at me.

"Don't do that!" he says. "Take my words and twist them into something else. I'm sorry I didn't get in touch. I wanted to, but . . . but I wanted to wait until I had a bit of money first too. To prove that I can make money and take care of us. Don't you think I've noticed that it gets on your nerves paying for everything, even though you say it doesn't? It's not as if I've been having the time of my life in Canada."

I think of Jordana. But not even under the most brutal torture would I consider admitting to him that I flew to Canada
to look for him or that I saw him with her.

"You want me to talk about my feelings and stuff," Ben
continues. "You want everyone to behave as you want them
to do in your head. Why don't you write a little script for us
so we know what we're supposed to say and do? Huh?"

For a few seconds, neither of us says anything. The storm
between us has abated a little.

"Actually, that wouldn't be so bad," I say in the end. "Perhaps that way people would stop disappointing me."

"Grow up," he says, but without as much rage in his voice
as before. "You don't actually want to be with someone like
me, you want to be with some Austrian banker."

"An Austrian *banker*?"

"You said it yourself. You only got together with me because you had no other choice. I remember you saying it on
the Donauinsel. Your biological clock was ticking."

My mouth gapes in surprise before I'm able to answer.

"Ben," I say. "That wasn't what I meant at all, and I *never*
said anything to you about any biological clock. I can't believe you've been thinking all this time that I was only with
you because of my age. And I'm not even old!"

Ben seems to be processing what I've just said and neither
of us says anything.

"I've come halfway around the world for you," he says.
"Do you get that? I've left my family for your sake. I don't
even like Vienna that much, but I'm still here. For you."

And I flew halfway around the world for your sake, I
think.

"Were you even faithful in Canada?" I ask.

At first Ben doesn't reply.

"I guess there were a few girls who tried, but I was only thinking about you the whole time," he says at last. "I really only wanted to make a bit of money. Money for us."

"But why couldn't you get in touch with me?" I say. "Like a normal person? Didn't you think I'd be worried? Did you think I'd wait forever? I just don't get your logic. Please Ben, help me understand what you were thinking."

"Of course I was always thinking about coming back!" Ben says. "I wanted to be back here with you the whole time! I didn't *want* to hang out with the old gang at the Drive and Donny's. Everyone's doing exactly the same things and taking the same old drugs as they were before I went to Europe. Stewie's still overdosing every weekend and Fat Reggie still goes looking for fights with strangers every time he gets drunk." Ben sighs. "I don't know why I didn't try to contact you again. In my head I have a bunch of explanations, but now I realize how idiotic they are. I really did go away to show you I could earn money and do my bit. You're the only person who's ever believed in me. Who's believed I can make something of myself."

I shake my head.

"But I don't any more," I say. "You're a loser who's never going to amount to anything. A slacker. Like Matthias."

As soon as I mention Matthias, I see Ben's shackles go up.

"Don't compare me with that asshole," he says angrily. "I'm not like him."

"You're *exactly* like him," I say. "Get. Out. Of. My. Flat."

44

Vienna's very first plasma donation center has opened on Kirchengasse. Since it's on the way from my apartment to the school, I've been observing the signs advertising the launch with excitement—and now they've finally opened. I go in on the first day.

"Welcome to the Baxter Plasma Center," the girl behind the white desk says. "Are you here to donate plasma?"

I nod and smile. Everything around me is white: the floor, the furnishings, and the ceiling. Just one of the walls is painted orange, and some of the furniture has orange accents. Enormous indoor palms adorn the corners, and everything feels airy and futuristic.

"Have you donated plasma before?" the girl asks, giving me an application form to fill out.

"No," I say, and the girl looks almost relieved, which is a little perplexing.

To tell the truth, I'm not even 100 percent certain what plasma is, aside from it having something to do with blood. But since the Baxter Plasma Center pays no less than fifty euros the first time you donate, and twenty each time after that, I don't care too much either. What's more, it says in their brochure that you can donate up to fifty times a year, which means I could earn over a thousand extra euros a year if I become a dedicated plasma-giver.

While I'm sitting on one of the orange chairs, I read that plasma is what's left over after all the blood cells have been removed without the blood being allowed to coagulate, and that it has important clinical applications. I carefully fill in the form and give it back to the girl, together with my ID card and a copy of my *Meldezettel*, the Austrian residence registration card. Almost immediately I'm ferried onwards, as though they're worried I'll change my mind. Then I'm asked to sit in a comfortable plastic reclining chair in a large room together with a dozen other people, while a woman in white puts a needle in my arm. Fascinated, I watch as my blood flows through the plastic tube and turns into a yellowish liquid in the whirring machine beside me. As I'm lying there I remember the call for new choir members at the church in Kaiserstrasse, and remind myself to email them as soon as possible to register my interest.

I lie still for almost an hour and a half, until they've taken enough of my plasma. I read a couple of magazines, and sneak the occasional look at the others in the room. When I'm done I get a Band-Aid for my arm, a piece of dry chocolate cake, and a new, uncreased fifty-euro note, and I think about how, with this new plasma-donation routine and the church choir, my future has never looked rosier.

45

As I'm coming out of Berlitz a few days later, I hear a voice: "Spare a little change for the homeless?"

I turn and see Ben sitting against a building. He's holding a paper cup from McDonald's. At first I say nothing. I'm happier to see him than I want to admit.

"You shouldn't give money to beggars," I say in the end. "Then they won't survive when they're released back into the wild."

I notice he's wearing new, unpatched clothes that I don't recognize.

"How come you're still in Vienna?" I ask.

"I live here now, whether you want me to or not," he says. "And I've signed up for a foundation course in mechanical engineering."

I decide not to tell him I knew he'd been accepted to the course six months ago.

"Are you going to be an engineer?" I say in a slightly sarcastic tone that I immediately regret because it makes me sound like I'm thirteen.

"Yep," Ben says. "I've already been to a couple of the

classes. The other students' voices have just broken, so it's like I'm their grandad. But the teachers are really cool."

"So what made you come over to the other side?" I ask. "I thought you were happy plastering walls and picking earthworms and living outdoors."

Ben ponders a while.

"Stinky feet," he says finally. "I don't want to be someone who always comes home with stinky feet, because then you know someone has a shitty job. And you probably had something to do with it as well."

"How are you going to support yourself? While you're studying?"

"I've got a job as a porter at the university," he replies. "It seems they constantly need benches, chairs, and books moved between different departments. And the job is legal and everything. I'm even going to be paying taxes now."

"And you haven't burst into flames yet?" I say. "Where are you living then?"

"Not in a bush in Stadtpark, anyway," Ben says with a smile. "I'm renting a little room in the fourteenth from a guy I thought was named Bogdan until he said after a month," Ben goes on with a Balkan accent, "'Ben, please stop calling me Bogdan. My name is Bora.' I could have sworn he was called Bogdan. I want him to be called Bogdan. He *should* be called Bogdan."

"Everyone needs a Bogdan," I say.

We both smile and fall silent for a while. Ben suddenly rummages for something in his pocket.

"I've even got a phone," he says. "Take my number."

Out of politeness I put his number into my phone. We fall silent again.

"I have to go," I say in the end.

"Meeting your Austrian banker?" Ben asks.

"Unfortunately, my Austrian banker is too busy exploiting the poor," I say. "But on the other hand, he does have a BMW and he buys me fur coats every day. Those ones that are made from lamb fetuses."

"But I bet he doesn't have a Bogdan," Ben says.

I shake my head and smile.

"Honestly though, where are you going?" Ben asks.

"I'm going to sing in a church choir," I say, throwing my arms wide. "Ta-da: new person!"

"Can I come too?" Ben asks.

"You want to join a choir?"

"God no," Ben says. "But I can wait until you're done?"

Suddenly my heart seems twice as heavy.

"It's probably not a good idea," I say.

Ben stands up.

"I want to apologize," he says. "Because I was so bad at trying to get in touch with you when I was in Canada. It was stupid, and I realize how sad I must have made you. Sorry."

"Thank you," I say.

"That said, I don't care how angry you are with me right now," he goes on. "I'm going to wait. You can't get rid of me that easily."

An image of Jordana and Ben outside Donny's pops into my head.

"Ben," I begin. "I'm never going to be able to trust you

again so there's no point in us being together. I need to be able to trust my partner."

Ben looks at me and his jaw tenses again. I'm unable to make eye contact with him.

"Don't say 'partner,'" he says in a low voice. "It makes us sound like cowboys."

"Goodbye," I say and start to walk quickly up the street.

As I try to swallow the lump in my throat I think about the choir to cheer myself up. In less than half an hour I'll not only be meeting a load of exciting new people, I'll also be singing beautiful songs and be spiritually enriched by doing so. I was wrong in Canada. You don't need anyone to share fantastic experiences with in life.

I'm the only one under seventy-five. In the ice-cold Catholic church Zum Göttlichen Heiland I stick out a mile in the flock of wrinkles, liver spots, and cataracts. I'm at least forty years younger than the next-youngest person there. I'm also Swedish and, in actual fact, Protestant.

"*O, ein neues Chormitglied!*" several people exclaim when they first see me, which makes me think it must have been a few years since the choir got a new member.

Everyone looks at me before turning to kiss each other on the cheeks or take off their coats. Everyone is well dressed and some even look dressed up. One elderly man is wearing a cravat, and several of the women are wearing elegant scarves and oversized necklaces. Around us, the church is full of the kind of heavy, gilded ornaments and statues of saints with empty eyes and serious mouths you always find in Catholic churches. Everything is wreathed in the scent of dust, perfume, and incense.

"Are you an alto or a soprano?" the choir leader asks.

"I actually don't know," I say. "Is there some kind of test I can take to find out?"

Apparently there isn't, since the choir leader just waves at me to stand somewhere in between the altos and sopranos. Because it's so cold in the church that I can see my breath, I keep my jacket on. When everyone is gathered, we spend ten minutes doing a few warm-up exercises for the voice and body, before the choir leader stands behind the piano and starts looking through a heap of papers.

"We're going to begin with a new song today," he says. "Who wants to do the solo?"

"Me!" I immediately shout, flinging my hand up.

Everyone turns to stare at me.

"That was a joke," I say quickly. "I don't even know what I am."

I forget to add that I meant alto or soprano. Only one of the basses laughs, so I decide to keep quiet unless it's time to sing.

"*Der gute Hirte leidet für die Schafe . . .*" the choir leader begins to sing, and we follow.

Singing in a choir turns out to be much harder than I thought. Firstly, I can't read music, so I have to listen to the others, and secondly, it's actually physically demanding. My jaw starts aching after half an hour, and singing, in all seriousness, about angels seems rather silly. The other choir members continue to look at me with curiosity.

"What a beautiful young lady," a man says when we've finished, taking my hand and patting it.

His hand is incredibly dry, and bearing in mind that his glasses are a centimeter thick, I don't know how seriously I can take his compliment.

"Where are you from?" the man asks.

"Sweden," I reply, and everyone around me bursts out in happy little "oh" sounds as though I were the reincarnation of Christ.

"But what are you doing here?" a woman says.

"You mean in the choir?" I ask a little nervously. "I'm Catholic," I lie.

"In Vienna, I mean," says the woman.

"I just really love Vienna, to be quite honest," I say, and once again the group around me gives its approval. If they weren't all suffering from back problems, I get the feeling they would have lifted me up on their shoulders and formed a procession—that's how glad they seem to be about the choir's newest, and moreover youngest, member. But instead I shuffle out with them all, already looking forward to next week's choir practice.

On the way home, I start wondering whether there's a hidden goldmine of other pensioner's activities for me to discover, and whether all these elderly people can perhaps become my new friends.

"I fought in the war," they'd tell me, tears filling their eyes.

"Me too," I'd say. "Or at least, I've seen a lot of films where people fought in the war."

"The bloom of youth is wasted on the young," they'd say.

"I agree," I'd say. "But really, what's the secret of life?"

And then they'd tell me.

When I'm almost home, an elderly gentleman suddenly stops me outside the haberdashery shop that's always closed. His jacket looks worn and dirty.

"Excuse me, do you have a cat?" he asks.

"Yes," I say.

The elderly man starts fumbling with a plastic shopping bag and gives it to me. I take it from him, unsure what it is he wants.

"My cat died," he says. "Please, take this."

I look in the bag and see some cat food and a couple of cat toys.

"But . . ." I begin. "Don't you want to get another cat?"

The elderly man quickly wipes a tear from the corner of his eye.

"No," he says.

And then he walks briskly down Kaiserstrasse and I see him wiping his eyes again. I look in the bag again and see the cat food is the cheaper kind, and that the cat toys look worn. I see too the lonely, cruel reality of old age.

~

"Please Optimus, just taste a little," I say when I'm back in the apartment. But Optimus refuses to eat the elderly man's cat food or to play with the toys.

46

It's my first evening class at the university. Apart from the fact that I've had to buy my own pens, I'm impressed by the modern buildings and, more importantly, with my hourly wage compared to what I get at Berlitz. While the students are coming in, I greet them and shake hands. Everyone smiles broadly and I try to remember as many names as possible: Özlem, Zsofia, Agi, Sunita, Fuat, Ahmed, and so on.

"Julia," I say, extending my hand to the slightly older couple who've just come in. They are both quite short and the woman is wearing a veil.

Shyly, the woman mumbles something that sounds like "Bahar," and shakes my hand quickly and weakly.

When I turn to the man he smiles and says, "Rahim."

I continue to hold my hand out and think Rahim might not have seen it.

"I'm a Muslim," Rahim explains in German.

I still don't get it, and a few strange seconds follow, before Rahim suddenly takes out his phone and I shake hands with that instead, while he holds the other end. Because I'd shaken hands with two Turkish guys a moment before, I'd completely forgotten that some Muslims don't shake hands with members of the opposite sex or with non-Muslims. Both Rahim and I are now obviously embarrassed, but luckily, some more students come into the room, so I can turn all my attention to them.

"My—name—is—Julia," I say as clearly as I can, once all the students are gathered and checked off in the register. "What—is—your—name?"

Twenty-one faces look at me with broad smiles and wide eyes. The group is Level One, which means they are all beginners without previous knowledge of the subject. Their backs are straight and their body language is still full of pure enthusiasm, which I know will start declining around the third week. I walk up to the first student, a young Slovenian woman with heavy bangs.

"My name is Julia. What is your name?" I ask.

"My name is Agi," she says.

I point at myself to indicate that she should ask me the same question.

"What is your name?" Agi asks me.

"My name is Julia," I say, turning to the next student. "What is your name?"

Slowly, we make our way around the room, and everyone gets to say their name. Over the following two and a half hours, we go through the English alphabet, the days of the week, how old the students are, and which countries they are from. My hand starts to ache from writing on the board so much, and my feet from all the standing. At nine o'clock, the lesson is finished and everyone leaves. Most of them look visibly tired, but everyone smiles and says a friendly goodbye.

When I've turned the lights out and am on the way to the tram, I call Rebecca to tell her I've just shaken hands with a mobile phone for the first time. But she doesn't answer, and as I'm sitting on the half-empty tram I start to feel horribly sad that I don't have a single person to share my story with.

47

Goodbye," I say to the woman behind the white desk.

"Until next time," she says, and smiles.

In my hand I'm holding two chocolate cakes, which I convince myself must be an indication of my enhanced status at the plasma center.

When I come out onto the street, I knead my inner arm and have to stop for a moment. I've been giving plasma almost every week, and have noticed how much weaker and paler I've become lately. Going to the gym has become a real struggle, and it is taking me longer to climb stairs. The other day, the old lady on the third floor went up the stairs faster than me. But I tell myself it's a small price to pay for saving the world and having enough cash to buy the fancy cheese at Billa.

I look at the clock and see it's only four-thirty. It's a bit too early to go home yet, and there aren't any exhibits or films that I want to see. Then I suddenly remember seeing an optician in the ninth district advertising free sight tests, and I immediately start walking there.

But just before I walk into the optician's I stop short. How many sight tests can I actually do? How many hearing tests? How much plasma can I give and how many times can I re-organize my books to fill the time? Is this how I want to live, until I die? I stand there for a long time with my hand on the door, until a bald man in a white lab coat waves at me to come in. I shake my head and walk away.

48

For once, Leonore and I haven't ended up at Passage, but at some dark club in the first district. The club is in a basement and consists of a bar and a tiny dance floor. Usually I'd refuse to be seen in a place full of older men buying champagne for giggling teenage girls, but this evening I don't care because I just want to get drunk and dance.

Leonore is standing, talking to a man by the bar so I'm dancing on the little dance floor. Beside me, two women in their forties are bouncing around, apparently desperate for one of the men around to notice them, but they're only paying attention to the younger meat in the room. At that moment, the DJ is playing Take That's "Relight My Fire" and a guy starts dancing beside me. His dark hair is slicked back, and he looks like he could have an Italian background.

"You like this song?" he yells in my ear in German.

"Of course!" I yell back. "Take That is totally underrated."

The guy gives me a thumbs-up sign and we go on dancing next to one another.

"What's your name?" he asks.

"Julia," I yell. "And you?"

"Bastian," he says.

"Like Schweinsteiger?" I ask.

"What?"

"Like Schweinsteiger, the footballer?"

The guy nods and gives me another thumbs-up. The DJ changes the track to "Born to Be Alive" and we start to get more physical. At one point, he rests his hand on my stomach for a long time, which I actually don't like, but let happen.

"Come on, let's get a drink," he says after a while.

We sit down at the bar, sweaty, but the guy gets up again almost immediately.

"Bathroom," he says.

"Sure," I say.

He vanishes, and suddenly I realize I can no longer see Leonore, which means she's gone home and left me here. I carry on waiting for the guy to come back, but he doesn't reappear. I carry on waiting and waiting and in the end I forget who I'm waiting for. I drink more vodka tonics and carry on waiting, because I'm hoping that if I just wait long enough the one I'm really waiting for will finally show up.

Suddenly I realize who that is. The one I've always been waiting for. I get out my phone and send a text, grab my jacket from the coat check, leave the club, and run towards the nearest metro station. During the twenty-minute journey I look out at the sun, which is creeping over the roofs to start the new day, and I think of the elderly man quickly wiping away his tears for his dead cat. Then I remember a warm, autumn day when two people with their fingers entwined lay side by side on the banks of the River Danube and laughed at a joke only they understood.

I'm the only person who gets off at Neue Donau. Apart from two men sleeping in the grass by the river and a man taking his dog out for a walk, the Donauinsel is completely deserted. But I can see that Ben is already standing there, on the pedestrian bridge. He's smoking a cigarette and looks almost surly, though I know his expression will change as soon as he catches sight of me. At the very same moment I step onto the bridge, all the streetlights across the island go off with a little sigh of relief. The rising sun has turned the sky from purple to a cool pale-blue.

"Ben," I say.

He turns to me.

"Hi," I say.

"Hi."

I nod at a rusty blue bike that's leaning against the railing. "Is that yours?"

"Yep," Ben says. "It's the Blue Bandit, Bogdan's old bike."

"What happened to your little kid's bike?"

Ben looks serious.

"Don't you remember, I'm a grown-up now?" he says.

"It got stolen, didn't it?" I say.

Ben laughs and nods. We're both quiet for a moment. Nearby a couple of gulls start squawking.

"When I said I didn't have any choice when I met you," I begin, "I meant because you're the most incredible, unique man I've ever met. Even though you were smelly and homeless and had dirty feet. I didn't want to be with anyone but you."

Ben doesn't say anything, he just looks at me.

"I'm ready," I say. "Are you?"

"Always," he says, smiling.

We kick off our shoes and climb over the railing, stopping on the little ledge covered in bird shit. The water looks incredibly far down, which makes my stomach contract, and I have to take a tighter grip on the railing behind me. Cool air streams up from the river.

Ben looks at me.

"Are we really going to do it?" he asks.

I look at him and nod.

"Yes."

"OK, but only if you promise never to make me go to the theater again," he says. "Or force me to watch *Harold and Maude* again. Because that film was really disgusting and should be banned. Or any Swedish films. Ever."

"I promise," I say. "And as long as you never force me to go rock climbing or do any sport that starts with the word 'extreme.' Or any sport at all."

"I promise," Ben says.

I let go of the railing and reach my hand out. Below us the Danube continues to flow.

"Then I think we can do this," I say.

"Of course we can," Ben says, taking my hand.

And we jump. Together.

ABOUT THE AUTHOR

Emmy Abrahamson debuted in 2011 with the young adult novel *My Dad's Kind and My Mum Is a Foreigner* (*Min pappa är snäll och min mamma är utlänning*). She has written three other YA books, and was nominated for the August Prize for *The Only Way Is Up* (*Only väg is upp*). *How to Fall in Love with a Man Who Lives in a Bush* is her first adult novel.

Insights,
Interviews
& More...

✳

A Conversation with Emmy Abrahamson

How to Fall in Love with a Man Who Lives in a Bush *is based on the true story of how you met your husband. Which aspects of the book diverge most greatly from your real-life experience? Which ones are closest?*

Just like Julia, I lived in Vienna for many years and worked for Berlitz teaching English while dreaming of becoming a writer. Elfriede Jelinek wasn't my neighbor (though she did live only one block away from me), but I have always felt like we would be really good friends because we share the same birthday (that, and the fact that I am almost a Nobel Prize winner). Julia is an extreme version of me—I would like to think that I am much more easy-going than she is—even though I also do love paying bills and color-coordinating my books, just like she does.

But I have also changed some details to give the story a better flow. Vic and I initially met in Amsterdam, actually. I was there for work when he sat down on the bench next to me, and then when I had to return to Vienna a week later, I didn't know if I was ever going to see him again. Vic had my mobile phone number but he didn't have a mobile phone or email address (and the Dutch postal services would probably not have accepted any letters to "The gorgeous guy who lives in a bush in Vondelpark, Amsterdam, the Netherlands"). But two weeks after I returned to Vienna I got a phone call and it was Vic saying, "I'm here now." He had followed me to Vienna and we have been together ever since.

One of the other big divergences from real life is that Vic never disappeared to Canada like Ben did (he would never behave like that!). Although Vic did end up going back to Canada for a few months, it was planned and I even came to visit him there. But writing about how "Julia and Ben went to Canada together and ate lots of nice food in Vancouver" just wouldn't have been as exciting. Oh, and I would NEVER jump off a fifteen-meter high bridge in real life. I'm not crazy.

What are the challenges for you of writing of an adult novel after a career spent writing for young adults? What are the most exciting parts?

The most exciting parts are being able to write about things like sex, masturbation, alcohol, and how mind-numbingly dull work can be. But I never really see my books as "YA" or "adult," and there is no difference in how I write them, only the subjects that I write about. A story should always be told well and entertainingly as possible no matter how old the readers are.

Julia is a frustrated writer who can only find inspiration in stories that already ▶

A Conversation with Emmy Abrahamson
(continued)

exist. Which writers have inspired you the most?

My life changed the first time I read Melissa Bank's *The Girls' Guide to Hunting and Fishing* in my early twenties. It was the first time I read about a female protagonist who was both intelligent and funny. There are quite a few books with strong women but they always lack a sense of humour (yes, I am looking at you, Katniss and Hermione, over there in the YA section). And if a female character is funny then she is usually a fat, ugly, or bitter secondary character. I found Bank's book wonderfully inspiring, and I always try to make my female protagonists both funny and smart just like she did. There is great power in humor and it is a fantastic tool to use when dealing with life's more difficult situations. I also love that Bank's book deals with loneliness so well.

Many of the characters in this novel are expats or immigrants. What do you see as the benefits of living in another country? What are the drawbacks?

I think everyone should live abroad for a while. You always feel like you are on vacation and get to see that there are many ways you can live your life. I also firmly believe that you can become who you really are abroad: no one knows your past or remembers that embarrassing thing you did in high school. It's a wonderful way to reinvent yourself and become who you want to be.

The drawbacks are loneliness, not being able to make friends with people other than other expats, and being expected to eat confusingly small breakfasts—like a small dry biscuit or something similar—when you are in Italy.

What are you working on next?

My next novel for adults will be coming out in Sweden this year. It's about a female stand-up comedian who gets committed to a mental hospital for depression. The book combines my obsession with female stand-up comedians with my own experience of depression and getting committed to a mental hospital. It's a crazily funny book! Or funnily crazy book? And I also finally get to confess my secret love for Phil Collins in it. I am already busy writing my third book for adults, and have sold a film script I wrote in just seventeen days. Life is good. ∾

Being the Man in the Bush
by Vic Kocula

Just before I became homeless, I was living and working in Dundee, Scotland, a place I'd chosen because I was able to live and work there with my Polish passport (I'm a Canadian citizen). I'd spent almost a year in Scotland when I decided it was time to see the rest of Europe and travel around as many countries as I could. In the beginning of May 2006, I quit my job, packed my bag and caught a flight to Porto, Portugal with the friend—The English—I'd been living with. Our plan was to live like movie stars, sample the fine wines and fine cuisine as we made our way up the Atlantic coast. Our transportation strategy was to simply stand by the side of the road with our thumbs in the air and get picked up only by limousines filled with supermodels and the occasional Italian racecar. Our savings was around 200 quid, a few packs of cigarettes, and a couple of T-shirts.

After a few messy nights in a couple of night clubs and a meal or two, the 200 pounds sailed off into the beautiful Portuguese sunset and we had to ask ourselves the important question: what the hell are we going to do now? The answer was actually quite simple: just get back on the road, stick out our thumbs, and go on as planned. The only catch was that we were now homeless and broke. Who needs money? We had happiness. Isn't that what everyone has been telling us all our lives?

Sleeping rough is actually quite easy when you don't have a choice in the matter. You simply find an appropriate spot, roll out your sleeping bag, and go to sleep. If the weather is nice, you sleep under the stars. If it's raining, you sleep under a bridge. Living the vagabond life is a test of your own self-worth and you can learn a lot about who you really are. I have never felt as free in my entire life as I did then.

Finding food was an adventure during that time but traveling in southern Europe, especially in the rural areas, you can find plenty of sustenance just growing on trees. If The English and I were really hungry, we just went into a supermarket, ate whatever we wanted, and walked out the front door. I still don't understand how no one ever made a big fuss about it but somehow we pulled it off.

In the beginning of my homeless adventure, the plan was to travel, meet people, and have fun. We definitely saw many beautiful places and met a lot of interesting people. When you have no money, you keep yourself entertained by chatting with people. Because of the time I spent as a vagabond, I now have the ability to approach anyone at any time and talk to them with no hesitation or self-consciousness. When you give up all the comforts of regular life and become someone that people try to avoid becoming at all costs, you have nothing to hide. ▶

Being the Man in the Bush *(continued)*

You are who you are and you can't put up a wall of material objects and fronts. It's like standing in the middle of a crowd naked, there is nothing to hide behind. Another result of this is that you really see what people are made of. The reaction of the people that I met was almost always positive. When they realize that you have nothing, but you are positive, confident, and can laugh about your own situation, people feed off that and open up themselves. This was my favorite part of the experience and it's something I will keep with me forever.

Now as you can imagine, living on the streets, you also meet a lot of people who have severe problems. Some of them were mentally ill, some were drug addicts and alcoholics, and some had issues I never figured out. But I tried to learn as much as possible from all of the people I met, many of whom were amazing and caring people that I call my friends.

Unfortunately, after living in the streets for a while, drinking and drugs became an everyday thing for me. My appearance started leaning towards the dark side, with my clothes eventually in rags, and I started to smell like I hadn't showered. I started to spend the little money I got from busking on booze instead of food and it started to show. Slowly, I became an alcoholic and I had to get a little more creative in making money—the less said on that topic, the better.

Eventually, The English had to go back to Scotland and finish his master's degree. At this point I was alone but I kept traveling, except this time from city to city because it was easier to make money. I'd been on the streets for six months and wanted to test myself and see how far I could take it.

Looking back, I'm glad I didn't go home because if I had, I wouldn't have met Emmy. I first saw her in Amsterdam when she was sitting on a bench waiting for a friend. She looked so beautiful that I could not take my eyes off her. After staring at her for some time, I decided that I had to go and talk to her. At this point I was visibly homeless and smelly and didn't think that she would be too impressed. But you really get to see someone's true colors when you're a person that most folk try to avoid. After talking to her for about thirty seconds I realized that she was even more beautiful on the inside than the outside. We hit it off straight away and for some reason that I still don't fully understand, she agreed to meet me a week later on the same bench. The rest of the story is history (which you can read about in the book, of course).

Now my life is very different. I live in a house instead of a bush with Emmy and our two amazing kids. With Emmy's help and support I finished a degree in mechanical engineering and have an amazing job where I can be creative and solve interesting problems while sitting in a fancy office. I don't take any of these ▶

Being the Man in the Bush *(continued)*

things for granted because I always think back to the times where I was cold, wet, and hungry, trying to figure out where I was going to sleep and how I was going to get a few Euros for my next meal. ⟡

Reading Group Guide:
Discussion Questions for *How to Fall in Love with a Man Who Lives in a Bush*

1. At the beginning of the book, Julia finds herself stuck, creatively, professionally, and romantically. How does meeting Ben get her out of that rut? Do you think that getting unstuck in one aspect of your life helps you reset in others?

2. Do you have any friends like Leonore? Is it better to have a friend like her than no friends at all?

3. Is it true, in your experience, that opposites attract? Are Julia and Ben more alike than they are different?

4. Is there any truth in Ben's criticism of Julia's snobbery?

5. What do you make of Julia's decision to go to Canada? What's the craziest thing you've ever done for love?

6. What's the biggest positive effect that Ben has had on Julia? What's the biggest positive effect she's had on him? ▶

7. What is the symbolism of the bridge that they jump off of at the end of the novel? Why do you think that Abrahamson chose to end the book this way?